BLACK LIVES RISING

APRIL GLOAMING

Chiatulah Ameke

©2021 Chiatulah Ameke
Cover & Illustrations ©2021 Abe Lara

-First Edition

Publisher's Cataloguing-in-Publication Data

Ameke, Chiatulah
    Black lives rising / written by Chiatulah Ameke / illustrated by
    Abe Lara
ISBN: 978-1-953932-04-4

1. Fiction - General 2. Fiction - Short Stories 3. Fiction - Black &
African I. Title II. Author

Library of Congress Control Number: 2021933850

To the African Ancestors and their unimaginable sacrifice, wisdom, and power. Most think you are dead—but some of us know better...

CONTENTS

THE JOURNEY

It was my brother who introduced me to the Group. It was clear he wanted my opinion because their material was totally different to anything he'd ever seen before, and he valued my perspective enough to see if I felt the same. He's never done anything like that before or since, so I've often felt he was guided by spirit or our ancestors. I'm glad he did because the Group helped totally revolutionise how I see and define myself, for the better.

At that time, the Group was literally just a handful of people and not the fully fledged organisation they would become. When I first met them, I remember picking up the book they had on display that formed the cornerstone of their belief and practice. It was the spiritual system of the Ancient Africans who built the pyramids and temples of the Nile Valley civilisations but in a depth, cohesion, and detail that completely blew western Egyptology out of the water. I wasn't happy with the little I read that day because I felt a foreboding. I immediately sensed this information was the real deal and would force me to confront myself in ways that would be profound but painful—and who really wants to change?

I bought the book and studied it in detail. I was shocked. I was a reader and a seeker, but this was simply light years ahead of anything I'd read before or since. With its cool scientific analysis, startling revelations, and endless spiritual insights, it corrected western

Egyptology like a professor would a schoolchild. Where westerners had dressed up their guesswork, misinterpretations, and cultural arrogance as scholarly facts, this book was clearly the work of an African insider at the very highest level of esoteric initiation and practice.

The insider's book broke down scientifically how all white political, economic, and social systems were products of a people who had a divisive, anti-holistic mindset that inevitably produced genocides, vast spiritual wastelands, environmental Armageddon, and the factory of child abuse known as Christianity. European destruction of our civilisations, slavery, and colonialist divide and rule had devastated and scattered our legacy and us as a people, but here was a work that challenged us to rebuild our greatness with inner spiritual force that white militarism couldn't in any way challenge.

The book turned me into an ardent supporter of the Group. I attended all their classes, bought all their key texts, attended meditations, rituals, socials, fundraising, and commemorative events. I fasted at the right time, helped out with security, and stacked chairs at the end of meetings and classes. I even went to retreats in America for a couple of years running, mainly to meet the leader and author of all the Group's books to see for myself if he was the real deal or running some kind of sophisticated scam. He turned out to be a genuine master. He led rituals where we delved deep into trance, allowing some of us to be physical vehicles for the Ancestors to directly transmit their wisdom from the spiritual planes. They always urged us to treat our spiritual development as a burning priority. I was

10

excited and hoped one day we would all engage in spiritual warfare that would bring down the white power structure with awesome displays of spiritual prowess.

But as the years rolled by, I realised the powers I wanted would take many, many years of intense dedication, involving high morality and relentless self-discipline wedded to an unyielding program of meditation. It began to seem an almost impossible task, requiring a patience I doubted I had.

Before the Group, I'd joined black revolutionary and white militant organisations because I wanted battles that would damage or end white dominance. I'd left because of the relentless racism of the whites or the dead-end intellectual posturing of the blacks. But here in the Group, the battle was against our lower selves, and it was clear the only warfare that would make change possible had to start inside to allow the powers of our true Selves to rise. I wasn't sure I was up to the challenge. I hoped those who might be more developed and powerful than me would strike a visible, tangible blow against white power that I could take heart from, but nothing ever happened that I could see. And I wasn't privy to the vision of those at the top of the hierarchy whose spiritual depth gave them a serenity I couldn't share. My morale suffered. My impatience, never far from the surface, began to impact on my commitment. My attendance and meditation dwindled. I felt less capable of change and hence, power, which again lowered my morale in an ever downward spiral.

As the years turned into decades, I would visit the Group maybe once a year but saw dwindling membership and no great change. Some new faces had arrived, and the knowledge imparted in classes was still priceless, but there was little to indicate serious progress in their power or fortune—the Group still found itself unable to even buy their own building. For all these years, they had rented from a succession of community centres, forced to work around others' rules and hours. For all its esoteric knowledge and uplifting rituals, the Group seemed perennially broke and devoid of business savvy. I was still loyal to all they believed and stood for but felt a sense of frustration at their homelessness. I'd heard of Christians establishing beautiful buildings from scratch by pooling members' resources—why couldn't we? I was confused and despondent.

On the one hand, I surmised that the Groups' destitution and lack of progress was down to their lack of business acumen, with the backdrop of our exhausting daily battles for survival in a racist society, as well as the divisions and apathy white Christians and Jews had literally bred into our communities since slavery. But deep down, I knew a greater truth was at work.

I wasn't the only old timer who knew for a fact that the Group's leader had true spiritual power and could easily generate vast material wealth, but it was equally clear there was only so much he was willing to do. He taught that our challenges in the physical realm were vital. They existed to force a spiritual awakening that led to true power, and some had actually been chosen by us in the life before earthly incarnation to form key lessons on a journey we had chosen to take. I knew he felt it was not his right to take away those important challenges. Though his books and rituals were irrefutable evidence of truly astonishing knowledge and abilities that could conjure wealth with ease, doing so would remove the struggle in the wider membership that was key to its growth.

But I could sense no significant progress in the other old timers, no end to our struggle as a people, no let up from the constant attacks we faced as a community, and little hope that the wider members of the Group, or any quarter in our community, were generating power or light at the end of the long, long tunnel. Maybe that was the point. Maybe things had to get even worse. Maybe we had to be forced to change—forced by repeated failure and near total disaster to truly utilise the legacy of our Ancestors that some of us, finally, after countless lifetimes, now possessed. True spirituality, I realised, contained brutal, as well as beautiful, truths.

Like many members, I initially saw the Group as a shelter from the storm where perhaps we could pitch in our resources and turn the temporary into a temple, a permanent, grander place of safety and all manner of growth. But over time, it was clear the Group didn't develop as we had hoped; there was no real power beyond the leader, no plan or thriving businesses to engage in that could take us all to the next level. Perhaps we had expected too much, but the teachings had raised our hopes. The Group's failings were a bitter disappointment because, for many of us, there was nothing else out there, nowhere else to go. Many drifted away, including me.

I felt mixed feelings towards those who stayed. On the one hand, I was deeply impressed with their commitment and resilience. I was also deeply grateful their presence ensured there was still an organisation I could occasionally return to that performed the rituals I so enjoyed. On the other hand, I thought I detected a weakness in some who stayed that I couldn't quite put my finger on. Was it a disturbing resignation to live small? Or was it the lack of vision, creativity, and initiative that demoralised and ejected so many of us? Was it the petty, patronising behaviour in some leading members, a loss of humility in others, all hinting at their own failure, staleness, or fear of the outside world that being big fish in a small and struggling Group barely masked? I wasn't sure, but I'd always sensed some members, new and old, were shallow, perhaps even fakes. I couldn't shake the feeling that many who were so profuse in their Africentric airs, graces, and greetings wouldn't give a fuck about me in the white world outside. It seemed that outside and away from the heady, mini-Africa the Group tried to create, many barely knew or connected with each other.

But whatever the Group's failings, and that of some of its members, the cold fact that gnawed away at me was that I wasn't doing my spiritual work at home or in my life, which is the real arena. Outside of my workplace successes, I was hardly shaking up the world with creative endeavour myself. I wasn't challenging myself in any real way to fulfil my spiritual potential. I was afraid of hard work, of the pain of self-denial and self-discipline. Still, the feeling never left me that I was drifting aimlessly, wasting my precious incarnation.

I buried myself in the search for a good woman, at times treating it almost like a full-time job. The relationship with the mothers of my children had been disasters, leaving me bitter and cynical, happy to reduce some women who really cared about me to fuck buddies. I was forever on the hunt for fresh pussy that might distract and sooth the growing sense of futility and foreboding within me. I couldn't find what I was looking for because deep down, I knew I was running away from myself.

The death of a long-term lover from cancer really shook me. I was middle aged, yet it was only the second serious loss in my life. Moreover, her passing made me realise how much I had actually cared about and relied on her. One day, I took the opportunity to have a spiritual medium give me a reading in my home. He was surprisingly accurate, giving me evidence of her presence that I couldn't deny through information only we, as secret lovers, shared. From there, I was drawn into the world of spiritualist churches and mediums that took their beginnings from alleged mediumistic sisters in 19th century America.

I wasn't impressed. The music played at their services seemed stuck in those bygone centuries, and all the pictures of angels, guides, or heavenly hosts were overwhelmingly white, as was the membership. Worse, unlike the Group, there were no earth-shaking rituals held by magical candlelight, sweetened with trance-inducing incense where powerful ancient chants and deep, soul-stirring drum rhythms beckoned Ancestors to dance with and uplift us. They seemed quite satisfied with the sterility of their weekly services.

Their focus was on passively receiving evidence of the spirit world, not spiritual transformation itself. I found it empty, stale, and fucking boring. I never felt at home. I only stayed because of the regular uplifting messages I got from my family in the Spirit world. They often urged me to become a spiritual healer. But while I enjoyed being a recipient of healing, I felt being a practitioner sounded too long and involved, plus I didn't want to spend too much time around these people. But the messages kept persisting and insisting.

Eventually, I began a practical course on healing and immediately started getting extremely positive feedback from patients. It startled me. The feedback opened my eyes to healing as a potentially important new doorway to the deeper spiritual experiences I craved, experiences that I'd left behind with the Group. I found I really enjoyed the entire healing process of making clients feel at ease before allowing Spirit to come through me as a channel and then offering additional words of comfort and inspiration after. I felt some sort of spiritual purpose was rising to the surface. The church began to rely on me more and more, and I felt an increasing sense of responsibility and connection to my regular patients as well as new people, who began to actively seek out my help. But otherwise and on the whole, I still felt bored in the church, never quite settled, out of place in a sea of whites who were strangers to ritual and satisfied with nothing more than the hope they might get a message from the medium. That wasn't enough for me, so there was still an emptiness inside and out.

By now, I'd been lucky enough to meet a woman who shared my hunger for spiritual depth. But what was particularly significant

16

was how quickly she proved to be totally trustworthy and dedicated to our relationship. I tested her over time, in various ways, large and small, but often subtle and covert. It was shocking to me how even in bad times she raised her game and seemed to become even more loyal, loving, supportive, encouraging, and resourceful. Added to which she was dedicated to the need for me to achieve my spiritual and creative potential, a need and potential that she sometimes seemed to feel more powerfully than me. I found it strangely reassuring how she didn't tolerate my laziness or excuses yet remained utterly and increasingly devoted. But I couldn't get away with excuses forever. Her persistent intuitive promptings joined forces with messages from my Spirit family, now urging me to write. The urgings became chilling warnings of all I stood to lose if I didn't seize the moment, as well as visions of all I could gain. Eventually, I began to write seriously and consistently for the first time in my life.

Writing seemed to open up another portal to Spirit. It released thoughts and feelings that had festered inside me for decades. It added another sense of purpose. It fulfilled a long-held ambition to not only be more directly creative by writing, but to write things I'd never read before. It made me feel I was being of service to my Ancestors, that I was finally heeding them and channelling their insights. I could feel their encouragement and inspiration as my thoughts unravelled, finally unrolling like an old carpet wrapped tight for years, revealing strange patterns and designs.

I now have a stronger sense of being on a journey. For a long time, I felt a victim of forces outside of my control, that I'd missed the boat, and all I could do was ride out the storm and hope I landed on dry land. Now, I feel more in charge, that my destiny is literally in my own hands.

I've started to go to the gym again, to meditate more than ever before, to see things that only persistence can reveal. *I feel the power rising that I always wanted,* not least in the book you now hold. *I feel you are about to witness it.*

THE PUBLISHER

The publisher had read my book and wanted to meet in person. I was excited. This was looking like the break I'd been hoping for after years and years.

The building was a shiny glass tower rising high from the heart of the city. The lift to the offices offered a panoramic view over the busy streets for miles.

I was greeted in the large, plush waiting area by a receptionist, Rachel, who looked as if she modelled swimwear in her spare time. She gave me a professional smile and ushered me into an even grander meeting room. She introduced me to Mr Cohen—the Director himself. This was going better than I thought. He looked up from his reading material, took his glasses off, smiled, and extended his hand.

He didn't waste any time. "Your work has promise," he said, "but no one who wants to stay in business will touch it." My heart sank. "Then why am I here?" I answered. He gave a small, sympathetic smile, "To be honest, I wanted to meet you in person, to see if we could point you in the right direction." "What do you mean?" I asked, but I could see where this was going.

He said my work had guts and spirit, but it was way too controversial and would upset too many people. "You've taken the race angle way too far. Controversy sells, don't get me wrong, but what you've written will frighten people, will cause a backlash that no one will be able to control or predict. People don't want to read about blacks, generally—it's a niche market. But they particularly don't want to read about blacks killing white people, even if it's justified. It raises all sorts of issues no one wants to think about. I'm going to be brutally honest: they prefer to read about black people as victims, or as sidekicks supporting the main lead—usually white, preferably a hunky white guy who has emotional issues or a badass white girl they can cheer on. Our readership, in fact, *most* readership, is female. They want to fall in love with the hero, or root for the white girl to overcome tremendous obstacles. They want escapism, or at least the feeling they can relate to the characters. They don't want the bizarreness and the brutality you throw in their faces. It either confuses them or pricks their consciences—either way, it leaves them uncomfortable, and that doesn't sell. Readers want happy, preferably romantic endings, where things are tied up in a satisfying way. You leave them hanging with no safety net in a world they can't recognise or identify with. Listen, we work closely with Hollywood; they keep us afloat; they need stuff that sells; that's the bottom line, as I'm sure you understand. There might be a tiny niche market for your stuff amongst certain types, but it's not going to make anyone any money.

I looked at him, nodded slowly, but said nothing.

"Listen…" he said encouragingly, "be smart. Look at the black writers we have in house—their work is totally non-threatening.

They stay away from controversy and some of them make a reasonable living. They touch on the race angle where you hammer it. They're smart; they do it without upsetting people. They don't rock the boat; in fact, they never really question the status quo because they recognise they're part of it now—they need it. At most, they criticise it—gently. They want to make it better—not destroy it. Your stuff would create enemies, needlessly, with all the wrong people. Black writers here have the the freedom to do whatever they want, but their black leads don't frighten or kill anyone…and if they do, they get punished by the system, which is an outcome that makes readers feel safe. The black writers here are all great role models now. You could be too. They've learned how to write what sells, what will pay their bills; they write according to the styles and subjects we've researched and determined are successful, so they can have some sort of career. And if we think they deserve it, we'll pull strings and favours to get them awards. It is what it is. This is about business, not art, and the blacks here who've succeeded were smart enough to realise that. Think about it—I can see you've got a bit of talent here, but use your talents wisely, you can still help your community but in a way that works and in a style that gets you payment and recognition. You'll never make it otherwise—I've seen it happen a million times."

I admit I felt a little disheartened, but I wasn't quite buying what he was saying. He seemed to be working too hard to put me off. And there was no real reason he couldn't have said all this in a letter much shorter than his speech. Ultimately, a man in his position needn't have responded at all, much less arrange to meet me in person. It all felt a bit odd.

I took a moment to think, to carefully consider his words. Finally, I stood up, shook his hand and said, "You're right. It was always going to be a long shot, but I'm grateful for your time and thoughts. It's not often someone like me can get the insight of someone in your position. It's really put things in perspective and made me think about what I really should be doing with my time. I'm a qualified social worker, you know, and I've never really maximised the opportunities in that field like I should have. Thank you again." I don't know whether he bought it, but it got me out of the office without any acrimony, and I wanted him to be off guard to at least buy me some time if what I suspected was true.

As soon as I was outside and out of sight of the building, I found a noisy pub, went into the men's loo, locked myself in a cubicle, and called my neighbour. I asked her to take the spare key I always left with her and to check my flat.

"What am I looking for?" she said when she reached it. I asked her to look at the very bottom of the door frame. I'd stuck a single, virtually invisible strand of hair from the door across the few millimetres to the frame. It was broken, signalling someone had been in. It was a trick I'd learned from an old friend who did something vague at the MOD.

I called him up, but he wouldn't talk on the phone, so we met several miles away, at night, in a park. I told him about the day's events.

He said, "You're not a threat at present so don't let it go to your head, but their actions suggest they think you might be, further down the line—not directly, but as an influencer, not conducive to the public interest, stirring up hate, could trigger some nutters, that sort of thing."

"What would you do in my position?" I asked.

"Keep writing. My guess is you'll get more support than you might suspect, and from people you wouldn't imagine. They'll pretend to hate your work, but they want change as much as you do."

"Who's Cohen?" I asked—just as we were about to go our separate ways.

"Small fry, a wannabe useful idiot. It's his secretary that runs the show. She's their contact inside. Did you ever watch the movie *Get Out?* It's something like that."

...ct or device used to hold a door open or
..., or to prevent a door from opening too w...
e same word is used to refer to a thin stri...
oor frame to prevent air...
...to prevent air...

(INTELLIGENT BLACKS)

ALL DECENT AND FAIR-MINDED PEOPLE

Dear TV and Radio Editors,

I would like to thank you on behalf of all right thinking people for the fantastic work you are doing ensuring that your presenters shut down intelligent and articulate black people who want a serious discussion on race that challenges whites to change. We do not want to be challenged, we do not want to change, and we certainly do not want to make amends for so called historical or present day injustices.

Far too often, these intelligent blacks (IBS for short!) want us to look at our slave-holding history from the viewpoint of so called victims. The hundreds of heroes we honour that built and grew rich off the slave trade deserve every ounce of credit for laying the foundations of our prosperity. We do not require any 'fuller picture' from these troublesome blacks and their tiresome facts. Thankfully, your presenters do magnificent work interrupting, diverting, belittling and ignoring them with wonderfully patronising and condescending statements and questions. They often completely derail IBS points with beautifully evasive tactics involving irrelevancies, whitewashed history, and ridiculous parallels that are a delight to behold.

I'm particularly impressed with how your presenters often use a succession of quickfire questions designed to distract and inflame the IBS, so he or she forgets his or her original point and engages the presenter on false ground—a wonderfully Machiavellian manoeuvre. I also enjoy the use of mock outrage from your presenters that the listener, viewer, or black stooge we control is invited to join in. The interview then becomes a media lynching that has me in raptures. It serves as an excellent reminder of how we must never miss an opportunity to let viewers and listeners know that at all times and in all cases, we whites are the victims of their rabid political correctness. We must always send the message to all listeners and viewers that these blacks are not to be respected or trusted, that they are the enemy within who would destroy all we hold dear.

Just imagine if we allowed them to talk freely. I know you all share my horror at how the floodgates would open and the general public would hear, in unnecessary detail, of the failure of universities to even admit to, never mind tackle, racism, of how football, far from being a beacon of progress, is going backwards, of the frenzied rise of racism since Brexit, of how gun culture in America is intimately entwined with whiteness and white privilege, of the endless coups and assassinations instigated by the West to ensure control of Africa's resources, leaving millions in poverty, of how for decades, we have disproportionately excluded black schoolchildren, of how the criminal justice system exhibits racism at every stage from police to courts, probation and prison, of how the West has waged secret biological warfare against blacks, of how we stole, destroyed, denied, and whitewashed their legacy in Ancient Egypt, of how the Windrush betrayal is part of a bigger betrayal that keeps their countries in never ending debt, of how we ensure so many of their children end up in prison, of how we maintain burning injustices in jobs, housing, health, politics, and of course, the media itself. There's no end to what they allege and where it might lead, so keeping them quiet is absolutely paramount.

As we are all acutely aware, the IBS demand we take responsibility for our actions and our so called ill-gotten gains when all we want to do is to live a quiet life. Their arguments must be shut down; they are the thin end of the wedge. Allowing them to be listened to would lead to all manner of new demands that could eventually lead to a drop in our living standards that would be completely intolerable— this is the true injustice we are all trying to prevent.

After the final analysis, we all understand we must maintain the current order and hold onto our wealth, privileges, and advantages at all costs, no matter how they were gained. The excellent way you use your power ensures we can go about our daily business untroubled by their spurious notions of justice. For this, I cannot commend you all highly enough, and you have the eternal gratitude of all decent, fair-minded people.

Sincerely,
W.

THE LEGACY

Dear Charles,

My dear fellow—it was a pleasure to see you at the Professors' conference. I may have seemed evasive, but I wanted to give careful consideration to your question as to why we find ourselves on the cliff edge of extinction.

I could give the standard answers I have often given the press, my students, and fellow academics, but I've been troubled. I've been ashamed of my own timidity in telling the truth, a truth that many of us have known for years, and I suspect you do too.

We must face the harsh fact that it is we, as white people, who have brought the world to within a few years of irreversible climate disaster. It is we, as white people, who have repeatedly threatened humanity's existence. Remember the Cuban crisis and the countless other nuclear close calls during the Cold War? Our 'civilisations' thrive on war and the genocide of First Peoples. This stems from the utter bankruptcy of our culture, philosophies, economic, and political models. We destroy foreign democracies and undermine other viable models because they don't serve the white race and our elites. Collectively, the white race repeatedly threatens humanity and will continue to do so because our arrogance is our true religion. It is our populations that should be reduced, not the dark nations we are constantly trying to find ways to reduce and kill off, so we can live in relative comfort.

Let's face facts—the central conflict white nations have been engaged with for centuries is for the control over the people and resources of Africa. Everything else in our history and thought is secondary. This is because Africa remains the richest continent in the world in terms of the resources the rest of the world wants and needs for phone, computer, military technology, and much more. This is why we have never allowed black people to control their resources for the benefit of their people.

But the true secret aspect of the desire to control black Africans is our fear of the power of their spiritual culture, which we largely destroyed through slavery and colonialism. Black Africans developed a spiritual culture in the pyramid-temples of Ancient Egypt far more powerful than any weapon we could ever devise. But where we made our gods, money, and weapons of war, they built their society on the upliftment of the human spirit. Consequently, many in those societies were able to achieve feats that, to us, would appear god-like. Just one of the many hundreds of their techniques was able to allow Wim Hof to reach Mount Everest's death zone in just his shorts.

The only reason we gained power over the blacks is that, like the seasons, their cycle had come to an end, and ours was on the rise. And what have we achieved with our time in the sun? Wars, genocide, deception, slavery, destruction, and corruption on an unimaginable scale that now drag all into the abyss, again.

Even if we manage to avoid climate disaster, we're likely to repeat all the same mistakes we, as whites, always do when we lead.

Perhaps we are approaching the darkness before the dawn. Perhaps a new black cycle beckons on the other side where their true spirituality breathes life into humanity's true potential once again. Perhaps, perhaps not.

I don't know what the solution to all this is, but I know much of it lies with the blacks, who are largely unaware of their power and legacy. Most of them are lost to Christianity, which we were happy to sell them, as it clearly did nothing for us. We have to somehow wake them up. The irony is they'll believe us white 'experts' more than their own because of our centuries of brainwashing.

Let's start telling the truth.

Professor Templeton

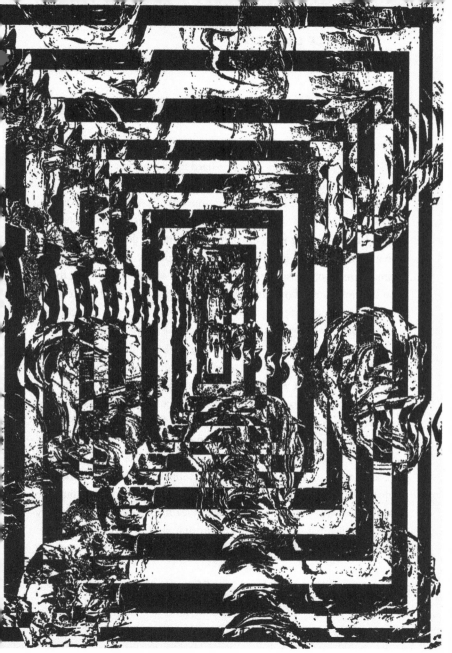

THE UNKNOWN SOLDIER

Mate, you're gonna find this hard to accept, but I just can't do the job no more. I don't feel right, and my head's not right. To be honest, I've felt like this for a long time but just put it down to stress, downed a few pints, and just got on with it. But it's much more than that. I'm wondering what the point is of what we do anymore. We've lost so many mates, good men, in so many places and for such a long time, I just wonder sometimes what it's all about. Are we just dying so the rich cunts above us can get richer? We were told we're making these places safe for democracy, to help protect our loved ones back home, but we seem to have made so many situations worse, and I can't see why we keep trusting these politicians who never send their sons and daughters to where we go. Isn't the history of the British army about working class idiots like us doing as we're told by the Ruperts who still shovel us shit once it's all over and whose upper class mates make millions either way? I just can't swallow the bullshit anymore when it keeps costing us so many good people.

You know what did it for me? Training those Western backed rebels in Africa who wiped out those villages, women, and kids included and destroyed that democracy in a filthy coup so that the Major General's in-laws could take over the diamond mines! Why the fuck are we getting involved in that shit? I've looked deeper, deeper than I wanted to, deeper than I've ever done, to find out that's what we've been doing for centuries—all over Africa and the world in the so called good old days of Empire where we 'gave so much to the world'—absolute bollocks! We massacred, stole, and covered it up; massacred, thieved, and lied; massacred and raped their people and lands for centuries to build our infrastructure, our cities, our industries, and created ever better weapons, so we could send our boys out to do it all over again! Our entire society is built on blood and lies and filth and betrayal of all the bollocks we say we believe in. It's blood money—all of it.

We, as soldiers, bought that shit and are the tip of the spear of all of it. As working class people, we should have been able to look at our history and know we were being lied to about the people we were killing and raping and stealing from. But we chose to turn a blind eye and switch off our consciences to feel part of something, to belong. But we were pissed on as grunts, and maybe it was our chance to piss on those we'd been taught were even less than us. We've forgotten who the real enemies are, what they've done to us, and the traditions, great traditions of how we resisted. I read somewhere that during slavery, the chain makers in England went on strike in solidarity with their black brothers and sisters being en- slaved in Africa. Why is it we only learn of that cunt Wilberforce and not our own who were starved out but held on as long as they could for people we had so much more in common with—we were being pissed and shat on by the same people! Where is that history? Why haven't we, as working class people, dug up and documented and celebrated that history instead of taking up arms in favour of those who hate us and show their contempt for us daily? Remember how many of us died in mobile coffins because the MOD couldn't give a fuck, and how we still die from countless PTSD suicides because none of them still give a fuck?

But we've got to take a hard look at ourselves and how we've allowed this minority to dictate to us the majority, and how they get us to commit the ultimate ignorant barbarity of fighting their illegal and immoral wars to make them rich. I'm so pissed off. But I'm still alive, so I can still do something different; I can still make my mark in a way that can't be ignored or misinterpreted. Well, at least I'll try. You're not going to like what I do; maybe you will after reading this, I don't know, maybe in your heart of hearts you'll know I'm telling the truth and will have a drink for me. I'm not claiming I know it all, but what I do know is that I can't be a pawn anymore in their game. We've all been used, and I'm truly fucked off with it all. Well, I'll be off now, and I can only wish you all the best. You've been a good mate, and we've shared a lot, but I have to go on this mission alone. It won't be easy to ignore what I've done—it will be world news. I'm head of security for a meeting happening right now of all the top Freemason bods in the army, Government, police, and legal types. Cunts, the lot of them—and they're about to be fucked.

WHAT I SAW AT THE MOVIES

I saw three films this month. The first was about the Holocaust. It was one of the most incredibly heart rending things I have ever seen. The bravery and resilience of the Jewish people were simply astonishing and brought me to tears several times. Their story is a true testimony to the enduring power of the human spirit. What they suffered is something none of us should ever, ever forget. We can never speak enough about this, and all related films, documentaries, memorials, books, exhibitions, and museums stand as a uniquely powerful legacy all future generations should continue to study. Together and always, we must affirm 'never again.'

The second film I saw was about slavery. Absolute bollocks. Why do the blacks keep fucking going on about this? It was years ago for fuck's sake; why can't they just get over it? I'm done with all this 'look what the white man has done' bullshit. Why should I feel guilty for stuff that had fuck all to do with me? We don't owe them a fucking penny.

The third film was again about the Holocaust. It was truly amazing, awe-inspiring, and thought provoking. It serves as a timely reminder to us all to redouble our efforts to support Jewish people everywhere in every way possible.

THE STRANGER

One evening, a stranger came to our home and said he wanted to tell us the truth about our son's death. Outside, men in dark glasses hovered, turning their heads slowly from side to side. Naturally, we were apprehensive and suspicious, but we were willing to grasp at anything, and when we insisted on recording everything on audio, he had no objections. After some small talk over coffee, I pressed record. This is what he said:

"We were very proud of ourselves when your Nathan joined our movement. He was a catch. We were a virtually all white group, and his arrival made us feel we were on the right path for potentially recruiting more black activists, as well as making us feel our attitude and behaviour didn't need to change. He burned with the same revolutionary zeal we did. He wanted radical action to improve the lives of millions—not endless debate. He loved the fact that we, too, wanted to get our hands dirty fighting racists and capitalists.

"Nat arrived when we were beginning to establish ourselves as the leading force on the streets. We started off targeting the far right, and Nat became our prize protege, someone we hoped would encourage scores of other young, angry blacks to join under our banner. We took him out with us on a few small jobs to test his mettle and initiate him into our ways and tactics. He graduated quickly from street fights against the far right and the police (often the same

thing) to leading sophisticated battle units delivering critical strikes against corporate targets in support of the environment and nationwide poverty. We developed a tech and media savvy political wing to reap the benefits of our class war.

"But two things happened at the same time: public support of our revolutionary tactics brought our electoral strategy to the brink of victory, and Nat had started to question our organisation's internal dynamics and the racial make-up and thinking of the top leadership itself. He said black people weren't involved at the highest level and didn't have a true say. He said the few blacks we had were mostly yes men there to make the organisation look good and encourage other blacks to make a difference—but only under white leadership and control. He said we didn't truly want to look at things from a black perspective, or to understand the impact and importance of black history, or to really understand how black people were still being treated across the UK. He said that our ideology was rooted in the flawed thinking of 19th century white theorists who saw black people as irrelevant primitives. Some began to agree with him and asked searching questions about how much we were really prepared to change during and after the revolution.

"We couldn't cope with his questions and the impact of his dissent. The leadership saw it as a cheek that he had the audacity to question them. He was speaking out of turn, above his station; it wasn't his job to think and strategise at a leadership level, or to question the sacred founding fathers of our ideology. Nat became continually surrounded by white comrades at all levels who vio-

lently disagreed with him. It was the familiar wall of white hostility, defensiveness, and arrogance when white leadership is challenged that so many black people I've spoken to since have talked about.

*"We attacked and undermined his arguments and contributions relentlessly. We began to write him out of our history. Nat came to be seen as a problem, and eventually **the** problem. Finally, he was condemned as a counter revolutionary who had to be eliminated to safeguard the revolution.*

"Nat saw long before we did that we were a product of and hostage to the ingrained white supremacist tendencies, habits, and traditions of white males in all Western political movements. The ultimate irony is that we shared much more in common with our capitalist and fascist opponents than we realised.

"I was ordered to perform the elimination because he trusted me.

"I left shortly after—many of us did, the guilt at our betrayal was too much. Eventually, it led to an internal war that tore our movement apart and allowed the capitalists and racists back into power. How we handled Nat destroyed the revolution that was within our grasp. We didn't realise then that we needed Nat, and others like him, to not only take us over the line, but to build a better future in the aftermath. Our white arrogance destroyed all we had built and all the potential for change we could have inspired nationally and even worldwide."

At that point, the stranger turned off the audio and rose to leave. We were still struggling to take in all that he had said when he turned and said his final words:

"Nat said for so long that Dr Ra Un Nefer Amen and Dr Umar Johnson were the only true legacies of Malcolm X and Marcus Garvey and would change the world in the way he had hoped we could have. We finally studied them and saw why. I can't bring your son back, but I can assure you that I and many, many others are prepared to give our lives to ensure they do."

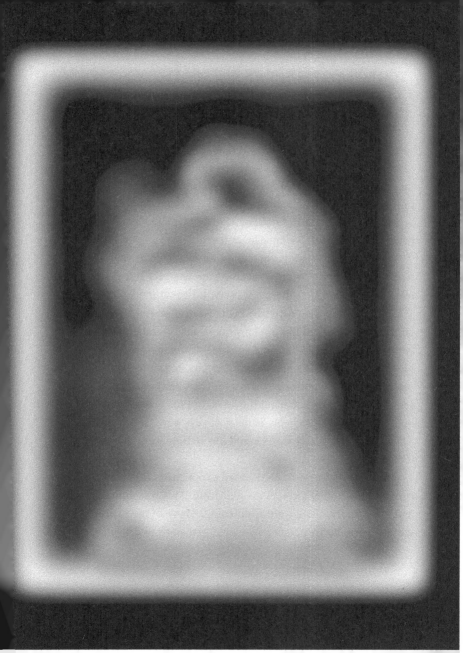

THE UNFORGIVEN

Even before I arrived, I felt something was off about the meeting. Rumour had it that it was about some unspecified terrorist threat. That seemed to be the most likely reason why we, as the most senior police officers in London, were being called to an emergency briefing by the Met Commissioner herself.

"Thanks for making yourselves all available at such short notice," she opened. "We just received the analysis from a specialist team at the Yard that there's a serial killer targeting our officers. We've lost 30 in the past year." There was a murmur of shock and confusion. We asked the obvious questions: was there any pattern; what was the race, gender, and age breakdown; had any motive been identified? She told us that the officers targeted so far were all white males between 45 and retirement age. The killings had been made to look like accidents and natural causes, but the analysts had worked out that the odds of so many in the past year were far beyond chance. There was no obvious motive, and the victims were drawn from all ranks.

Despite the years of hard-nosed experience in the room, I felt a ripple of fear travel through the gathering. This was unprecedented, and the numbers were truly frightening. Many of the officers killed were experts in all manner of special weapons and tactics, so the fact that even they could have been taken out meant we were all in danger.

The Commissioner continued: "We don't want to say how we've differentiated genuine deaths from the killings. And we don't want to alert the public yet in case we generate copycat killings— your good policing has created a lot of enemies out there. We're asking you, though, to brief all the officers under your command to be extra vigilant. I've secured extra funding from the Government to fast track taser training and provision for you all. The intelligence services, too, will be assisting in monitoring known suspects and helping to find any patterns that could lead to arrests. You'll all be issued with stab and bullet proof vests as well as personal alarms that will be at your discretion to use."

Given the level of sophistication it must have taken to engineer these deaths, I asked whether foreign or domestic military sources were being looked into. "We thought the same, Becky," said the Commissioner. "MI5 and MI6 are looking into this as we speak. GCHQ is already monitoring suspects, and we're co-ordinating findings. We'll find whoever's doing this, but we need you all to be extra vigilant in looking after yourselves and fellow officers."

A handful of us were instructed to stay behind after the meeting. For one awful moment, I thought we were suspects, but the Commissioner had other ideas. "We're pretty certain these murders are the work of an insider," she said. "All of you are close, in one way or another, to key suspects we've been tracking, some of whom were here today. Becky, we want you to take an extra special interest in your immediate line manager, Deputy Assistant Commissioner Terry Northfield." I was shocked. How on earth did Terry end up being a suspect? Northfield had been my mentor as I rose through the ranks, and I'd asked to be transferred to his department the first opportunity I got. He was a copper's copper and couldn't be more proud of his years and colleagues in the Force.

The Commissioner saw the shock and confusion work across my face. She explained that Northfield fitted the profile they'd drawn up: ex-special forces, Freemason, worked with several of the victims on his way up—there'd been the whiff of corruption over a few of the cases he'd handled back in the 80s and 90s, but nothing had been proven. "But what motive could he have?" I asked. "We don't know as yet," said the Commissioner, "but his alibi for a few of the killings doesn't check out, and he refused a polygraph." I knew Northfield would have refused on principle, outraged at the mere suggestion he was a suspect.

The Commissioner was halfway through briefing the others when her assistant burst into the room and said breathlessly that it was an emergency. We were told to wait. After only a few minutes, she returned with a grim look on her face. "Northfield's killed himself," she said. "He left a suicide note admitting his involvement in the serial killings." I burst into tears. We were sent home.

That night, my partner, Kwame, pulled me close. "You okay, hun?" he said.

"Yeah, just a little shaken. It was a close call today, but North-field did as he was told."

"Well, he didn't have too much choice with the child porn we had on him," said Kwame. "You've done so well, hun," he contin-ued, "Northfield teaching you all the tricks of the trade makes our work possible. The sex you had with him for all these years was worth it."

He was right. The case was closed, and I took Northfield's post in due course, and we continued the work we started 20 years ago, punishing racist cops. We were just a little more careful now.

THE DELIVERY COMPANY

Today's delivery was to a client in the country. We drove through large wrought iron gates and down a long, winding drive past lakes and fountains until we reached the doors of a huge palatial mansion where a butler was waiting.

We'd prepared 'Jeeves' the night before with credible threats to his family, so he knew how to behave, and he had disconnected alarms and cameras at the right time. We'd told him we just wanted to frighten his boss.

Upstairs, the whole family was dining around a huge table, Downton Abbey style. They looked a little confused when we walked in with our delivery uniforms and Jeeves in front of us looking strained.

Jeeves, his job done, took a bullet to the back of his head; there were screams and shouts as blood sprayed across their food before he fell to the floor. With these types, you never knew whether they're more worried about the food or the help.

The husband tried to be the hero by standing up and demanding what the hell was going on. A shot to the leg sat him back down and reasserted our authority.

We still hadn't said anything, but we took positions on either ends of the table to cover any false moves. There was only quiet sobbing to be heard from the females and moans from the guy we'd shot. The boys just stared in shock.

I nodded to my partner, and he began speaking. He said that in 1833, the British Government used 40% of its national budget to compensate slave-owners, not slaves, for ending slavery. And that the amount borrowed was so large that it wasn't paid off until 2015.

My partner paused. The wife intervened to say, "Please, what on earth has this got to do with us?" I came in at this point to say we'd obtained a list of recipients of this compensation, and they were on the list.

The wife looked at her husband in confusion. He, despite the pain of his gunshot wound, managed to look sheepish. His wife immediately realised the situation and offered us anything we wanted.

We took her up on her offer. Husband and wife helped transfer their entire savings to untraceable accounts we'd prepared with the help of a previous 'client,' sadly deceased. It was in the region of £100 million.

What will you do with us, they asked, now back with all the family in the dining room. I asked if they knew what the slaves behind their wealth had gone through so her family could live in such comfort—for centuries. Hubby was silent, the wife stuttered, struggling for the right words. "Listen, we are so, so sorry for what happened to your people," she said finally, "but we had nothing to do with it, and surely it didn't affect you, personally; it was all so long ago; surely, as a society, haven't we all moved on so much since then?"

I pulled out a piece of paper and read a quote from Malcolm X:

"If you are the son of a man who had a wealthy estate and you inherit your father's estate, you have to pay off the debts that your father incurred before he died. The only reason that the present generation of white Americans are in a position of economic strength is because their fathers worked our fathers for over 400 years with no pay... we were sold from plantation to plantation like you sell a horse, or a cow, or a chicken, or a bushel of wheat. All that money... is what gives the present generation of American whites the ability to walk around the earth with their chests out... like they have some kind of economic ingenuity. Your father isn't here to pay. My father isn't here to collect. But I'm here to collect, and you're here to pay."

I folded the paper away. I said I'm afraid Malcolm's words are entirely applicable to the UK, and yours is a particularly serious case. The payment must include your lives—and that of your family.

Half an hour later with the job done and loose ends tied, we drove back down the winding driveway away to meet our next client.

THE DIRTY TRUTH ABOUT BREXIT

The dirty truth about Brexit is that every class and section of white society has totally betrayed the black immigrants who sacrificed their lives to build this country. Brexit is a case study in racist manipulation and self-deceit that black people have seen a thousand times before.

The white working class, who should have been our natural allies, have gotten so good at betraying black people, they have turned it into a national sport. For decades, if not centuries, they have swallowed every ruling class and media lie, slander, and stereotype of black immigrants. In the army abroad and the police at home, they have long done the dirty work for the ruling class without question. They have betrayed each other as well as us and always stand to lose as much as, if not more than, us because of their perennial stupidity and short sightedness.

The white middle classes are the most two-faced and duplicitous of all the classes. They pretend to be our friends but write the articles that damn us and shut down debate on radio and TV when we try to discuss the truth. They are the managers who sack and disproportionately discipline us, they are the university academics who mark us down and keep us out, they are the council managers and landlords who ensure we get the worst housing, they are the senior police officers who sanction our harassment and abuse every day, they are the creative, tech, social work, political, and legal types so entrenched in their white privilege they can't see theirs, or any, racism anymore. Where the working classes have been conned into seeing us as rivals, the middle classes can only see us as servants. The middle classes might express sympathy to our faces but then urge our enemies to go in harder. They use words like 'regrettably' when they don't actually give a fuck. With their education, contacts, and access, they could have made a convincing and consistent case over the decades for the massive benefits black immigrants brought and still bring to this country—but they are weak, cowardly, two-faced cunts, so they didn't.

The ruling class benefits massively from the idiocy and cowardice of the working and middle classes. They control the minds and behaviour of the lower classes and profit either way, deal or no deal, leave or remain. They use royal propaganda as their main weapon. All the 'queen and country' bollocks is to maintain a vice like grip over the minds and loyalty of the lower orders. The rich rulers couldn't give a fuck about Brexit, queen, or country as long as they stay rich and can flee to tax havens abroad, should the masses wake up and truly revolt against them. But the masses never do; they never have, and they never will. So, black immigrants are within their rights to do whatever it takes to get back the stolen wealth that forced them to immigrate in the first place. Whites, of all classes, are having internal wrangles and tantrums but have always made clear they simply don't give a fuck about us, Brexit or not.

For Georgie

My Dear Son,

I won't be coming home today. In fact, I won't be coming home at all.

I'm in the hospital, surrounded by police, handcuffed to the bed. Something happened today. Quite a few things actually.

Me and your uncles and aunties just couldn't get over how the stress over the Windrush business killed your Uncle Georgie. You know how close we all are. He was the eldest and more like a father to us.

We had a few hours with him before he died. He was conscious and talking almost until the very end. We laughed and talked about the old days, how proud we were to come here. We saw ourselves back then as the cream of the crop and knew so many would be envious back home that we were in the 'Mother Country.' He helped keep us together and sane during the hellish torrent of racism that was poured on us wherever we went, whatever jobs or homes we applied for. Even the churches told us we had to leave as we were upsetting the other parishioners. Georgie helped us settle and survive for all these years. We've all given so much to this country for so long and he, the best amongst us, was trashed like used toilet paper. They couldn't wait to deport him. His heart attack stopped the deportation and gave us our last hours together. He spoke of you. He said you were right all along about this country, these people.

After he passed, we went back to his house. Junior, your cousin, was there, of course. He was mad with rage and grief. To be honest, we all were.

"Do you see now? Do you see now?" he kept on screaming.

"The police beat and framed me over and over again, and now the same system has killed dad! We kept on telling you what they were like, but you wouldn't listen!" We couldn't look him in the face. He was right. We had never properly believed or supported him as a youth. We didn't believe police could be so racist. Back home, we were taught they were the best in the world. We thought he must have done something wrong for them to keep arresting and harassing him. Windrush made everything that you and he had said for years so obvious. We had been so naive. We thought we were finally accepted, safe, integrated, valued. We were blind; actually, we didn't want to see, we wanted to believe we'd made it in the mother country, we wanted to be the envy of the folks back home. We thought we were the cream of the crop—but like you said, we're just niggers to the Government and to so many of this country's people. Labour and Conservative agreed our numbers needed to be controlled—like we were rats or vermin. Labour's betrayal was worse because we voted for them in droves for decades.

We forgot they had all made us slaves and profited from our humiliation and pain for centuries, and that we were in the belly of the beast. We got comfortable, complacent. We didn't want to listen to the younger generation. When deportations affected others, we stayed silent, considered ourselves safe and fortunate and forgot about them. I had been so proud when your uncle got his MBE, but now I know it is a badge of shame and disgrace. We had been forced to become Christians during slavery, but centuries later, chose to still cling to the myth of Jesus—betraying our Ancestors who, like you, fought that we might be free. What an abomination to take the slave-masters' religion and spit on the millions of graves and memory of our Ancestral family who died for us.

You and Junior tried to tell us all this. You and Junior were the ones who went on all the marches, to all the protests, joined all the groups, supported all the campaigns, suffered all the arrests, all the beatings—and we did so little. We cried our eyes out for our shame, for all our children who tried to tell us, for all our ancestors suffering, for Junior and poor Georgie.

Junior couldn't bear what happened to his dad. It tipped him over the edge—it tipped all of us. I don't know where he got so many guns, but there were enough for all of us. We held hands in a circle and said a last prayer, not to Jesus, but to Nat Turner, Toussaint L'Overture, Malcolm X, Garvey, Queen Nzinga, Yaa Asantewa, and all those great black African men and women you told us about who fought, bled, and died for us. We hugged, kissed, said our last good-byes and went out into the night.

The police say dozens, maybe hundreds, died, mostly police and politicians but some priests too. Your uncles and aunties are all gone. Junior's gone too. I couldn't go too far because of my knees, but I got a few of the neighbours—you know, all the ones who always looked at us with contempt ever since you were a kid.

I don't care what happens to me know. I'm proud of what we did. We all saw it as a precious chance to cleanse our shame. I can hold my head high and say that my life meant something—that I finally listened and understood and made them pay. I can look the Ancestors in the face and say I didn't disgrace them—that they didn't die in vain, and neither did beloved Georgie.

All my love always,

Mum

A Simple Truth

Every day some commentator castigates Trump for being sexist, racist, unstable, incompetent, corrupt, a danger to all, and so on. But all these commentators miss a simple truth: what else can you expect from a society that was built on slavery and genocide and refuses to apologise or make reparations for either?

Trump shows a glimpse of America's real face, its real racism, its real arrogance, hate, narcissism, ignorance, stupidity, denial, irrationality, and sickness. Everything the commentators criticise about Trump actually explains and reveals who America is controlled by and who America really is.

The commentators criticising Trump would have us believe that getting 'reasonable' people like Obama into power represent progress—but it doesn't and never has.

For example, Obama, like all other 'reasonable' presidents, continued the warmongering imperialism that threatens the entire globe, and presided over ever more naked racism in all the systems at home. He, like all the other 'reasonable' presidents, could do precisely nothing to fundamentally change America because they are all-knowing puppets of a white military-industrial-financial complex whose rape and pillage mindset is part of the very DNA of America. These are the true white supremacists, they hold the true power, and their appetite for violence is only matched by their capacity for deception and their pathological fear of a black uprising. This is why millions of black people were conned into thinking their votes for Obama would help ease racism when it did precisely the opposite.

So many people naively sat back, thinking that racism was over with Obama's election, when ironically, all it did was allow racism to flourish in every corner of society completely unchecked. They, and so many others, have all forgotten or ignored the fact that the white supremacist dynasties who control America have never apologised for, never mind offered reparations, for what are the greatest crimes in all humanity—and they never will. This is because they correctly see true justice and truth ending their power.

Urbane, sophisticated, and articulate Obama is how many Americans would like us to see them. Presidents like Obama are deceptive window dressing, hiding the fact that nothing has changed, and in fact, gets worse precisely because so many believe in the window dressing.

Will a new 'reasonable' president stop America's wars for oil and the rape of Africa's wealth? No. Will a new president pay the trillions of dollars in reparations to black people that are hundreds of years overdue? No. Will a new president offer even a fake apology for the uniquely barbaric slavery and genocide that built their nation? No. Will a new president stop the shootings of unarmed black men? No. But a new, 'good' president will see the many critics of Trump ready to sell the lie that things have changed so that the gullible can go back to sleep and America can continue its crimes against humanity and the environment worldwide.

The fact is, the endless deception and barbarity that defines America can only begin to be tackled by recognising this simple truth at all times.

THE WOODEN BOX

I don't think it was long after my father died, a few months perhaps. I still remember the fresh new sense of loss and vulnerability I carried with me at that time, like an invisible backpack.

Christopher's dad was a good friend of our dad, and he'd visited our house many times when my dad was alive. We didn't know his name, we just called him 'Christopher's dad' to distinguish him from other uncles because we were around the same age as his son, whom we occasionally played with. I was about 12, and my brother was a year older.

Christopher's dad came round one day, sometime after my dad had died, and asked me and my brother to build him a wooden box. It was likely he wanted to ship something to Nigeria, but we never asked, and he never said.

Me and my brother had never built a box before, but we were excited at the prospect of the reward that we would earn for being trusted with such a serious and responsible undertaking. It was likely to be up to £5, maybe each, which for us kids in the 70s, was a serious amount of money. So, we took the job on with enthusiasm and anticipation. He supplied us with the wood, and I think we might have used some of my dad's tools, as well as his, to saw and shape the box.

We measured, sawed, and hammered for hours before we finished it. We were tired and sweaty but very proud of what we'd achieved. It wasn't perfect, of course, but it was clearly a sturdy, if roughhewn, box that certainly looked like it would do the job.

So, the time came for our uncle to inspect the box, and he was pleased with our efforts. Me and my brother stood expectantly, broad smiles on our faces, waiting to see how much he would shell out for all our hard work. If we got a five-pound note each, it would have been a rich but fair reward for the work we put in. Even if it was £5 to share, this was certainly not to be sniffed at in those days, and we would have been happy.

We stood there tired but to attention, expectant, with our hands still sore and saw-dusted from our work. Our uncle spoke: "Well done," he said, "it's to your credit." And that was it. No money. No fiver each, or even a fiver to share, or even loose change. Nothing. Zero. He left with his box, and we stood there stunned and embarrassed.

I don't think we said much at the time, but for decades after, me and my brother turned it into a running joke we used on each other. If either of us reported any success or did something well, the other would say, "It's to your credit," and we'd laugh wryly. But that incident stayed with me ever since, and I know it affected me deeply. Until now, I've never really analysed it much beyond what we knew at the time: the bitter realisation that an uncle we trusted and respected had deliberately taken advantage of us.

Compared to other episodes of deception or abuse, some could share it doesn't seem to rank highly. But I now see that for me, this incident burned deep into my psyche because it represented several layers of betrayal: that of our young, innocent trust and again towards my father. And on an even deeper, painful level, his act confirmed and exacerbated the loss of our father. It was a reminder that Dad was no longer there, the strong safe presence to protect and defend us. No uncle would have dared to pull that stunt if he was. Dad was too strong, too outspoken, too respected and renowned. He was a protective, loving presence we knew we could rely on. But Dad was gone, and that uncle confirmed it, made it a harsh reality, and introduced us to a new cold order. I would have to survive without Dad when it had never ever occurred to me I would ever lose him. It was almost like I didn't know that people actually died—and then my first experience of it ended up being the pillar of my sense of security and safety in the world.

Perhaps a part of me had hoped that one of our many uncles would step up and be something akin to a fatherly, protective, guiding presence in our lives. Our Dad had so many, many friends. But no one ever did.

This incident made me lose a lot of my innocence and optimism about life. Looking back, I can see it hardened me, gave me a cold reminder that I was alone in this world. My innocence and vulnerability hardened through the years since then into a shield of cynicism, aggression, and bitterness, behind which the loss of my father always lingered.

Dear Rachel,

Sis, I know you're really proud of being Jewish, but I'm really struggling being a Jew at the moment. There are so many things going through my head. I've started to read a lot more than I've ever done and talked to a lot more people than I've ever done.

I just don't see anymore how we can call ourselves 'chosen people' when we treat Palestinians with such brutality. We're subjecting them to many of the indignities we suffered under the Nazis and viciously attack anyone who criticises Israel. I just don't believe anymore that God would choose us over anyone else, considering how we behave to others. What actually gave us the right to take another peoples' land? The British helped us steal another peoples' land for their own agenda—just like they've been doing in Africa for centuries. Let's just start telling it as it is. I read about one Jewish guy who said that Israel is the only country that can slaughter babies and still claim it is the victim. He lost his job, of course, amidst the usual manufactured hysteria that he was a 'self-hating Jew.'

The truth is we are white Europeans—our ancestral homelands are in Europe. We converted to Judaism en masse in Europe centuries ago and now claim a right to an Israel that isn't ours. We are white Europeans and as racist as those we condemn. The real Jews are black like the Falashas from east Africa, whom we welcomed to Israel in the 80s, only to throw away their donated blood because we feared they had AIDS and use their numbers to bolster the illegal settlements. And I've heard all the bollocks I can stomach about Israel being an oasis of democracy in the midst of a sea of Arab despotism. If I steal someone's house and build Shangri La on it, it is still stolen land! Many of the Palestinians we forced out of their own homes still have the deeds, for fuck's sake.

The reality is our actions fuel anti-Semitism and encourage conspiracy theories because we shut down genuine, open debate and ensure people lose their jobs if they do anything but sing our praises or sob over our stories. Our bullying tactics are so transparent, and we're losing far more people than we realise as a result. Most only support us out of fear, not respect. And for that reason, many hate us. They hate that they have to censor their thoughts and speech, hate that they have to censor their writings, their ideas, their creativity, their stories, their articles, programmes, books, speeches, lectures, messages, and everything that it is to be creative and free to save their lives, jobs, and families from our slick attack machines. And we train non-Jews to attack on our behalf, so they can prosper in the warped reality we have created where not to defend Israel and our every behaviour or word and action as Jews is, of course, 'anti-Semitism.'

It's so painfully obvious that the hysteria over anti-Semitism in the Labour party is manufactured by us and our minions across all parties and the media who have united with the ruling class to take Corbyn down because they hate him and because of his principled stand against Israel for decades. And this is unforgivable because Corbyn is a good man who would do so much for millions in this country and the issues of equality and racism we claim to care so much about. We destroyed Ken Livingstone, too, because he exposed the fact that Zionists colluded with the Nazis (read Tony Greenstein's 'Zionism and the Holocaust'—the truth is actually much worse than Ken said).

Our tactic is to destroy good people and put lackeys in their place. Morally, that makes us bankrupt. The Board of Deputies, in a joint public statement with a huge host of other Jewish organisations, declared Corbyn an existential threat to Jews—and in that instant not only revealed their true colours and utter lunacy, but pissed on the graves of Jews who died from real existential threats.

And it's not just the rabid Zionists who are fucked up morally and intellectually—scratch the surface of 'liberal' Jews who are 'not that into politics' but when discussing Israel, you very often find hardcore racism that attempts to justify, excuse, and downplay endless slaughter of Palestinians to protect Israel. They say, "Of course something should be done, and of course Israel has made some mistakes," but then do precisely nothing to stop the slaughter because secretly they support Israel regardless and believe the massacres are a price well worth paying. Meanwhile, many of us Jews suffer the backlash worldwide at injustices so blatant that children can see it.

Remember too when Ricky Gervais at some awards ceremony said to Kate Winslet that to get the Oscar she craved, she needed to do a Holocaust movie? I nearly died of embarrassment. Gervais let the cat out of the bag about how our control of Hollywood and the media allows us to disproportionately and undeservedly reward those involved with the endless promotion of our victimology. If I never see another fucking Holocaust or Nazi themed movie, it will be too soon. We can't claim to be powerless victims anymore. We can't claim to be vulnerable and then bomb countless defenceless women and children into oblivion with the very latest jets and weapons of war.

We rightly say, "Never forget," and Israel collects billions in compensation from Germany for what happened in the war. But a black friend pointed out that when black people try to talk about how white people benefited massively from slavery and colonialism and still do today, they're told, "It's all in the past," "You need to move on," and that reparations to black people would be patronising, too complex, and in any case, "Where would it all end?" As Jews, we never speak up about this—and I know why. It's because we were deeply involved in slavery at every level, and I found this out reading 'The Secret Relationship Between Blacks and Jews.' It's written by Louis Farrakhan's Black Muslims and uses Jewish sources for 90% of the book.

The book shows, in excruciating detail, how and where we got much of our wealth from and that we are deeply racist and have been for centuries. But we dismiss this truth as an anti-Semitic conspiracy, and we get so called experts to condemn what is so painfully obvious. If this book is anti-Semitic, then the phrase has no meaning anymore and is mostly a political tool for the repression of truth and justice. Read it for yourself and make up your own mind.

The harsh truth is that we conspire to suppress this knowledge of our wealth and racism. We can change our names to hide our identity. Our white skin allows us access and assimilate into key sites of power that would be impossible for black people to be admitted into—but whose cause we shamelessly use whenever it suits us and stay silent when we need them to provide a buffer for us in society. We prey on their culture and genius for money, power, and control and claim we are their friends, but now, as in slavery, we are disproportionately involved in profiting off their land and people in every possible way. Even at the end of slavery, we helped finance compensation of countless billions to slave-masters—because many of us *were* slave-masters.

In our Rabbinical texts, we describe black people as ugly, liars, lovers of theft, and condemned to be enslaved for evermore (read 'Hebrew Myths' by Graves and Patai). We describe God as angry, jealous, and ourselves as 'chosen' to justify our barbarism. Hitler would be proud of the brutality we have shown black people and Palestinians. We use our hold over academia to change history to ensure lies are believed and truth is discredited. We have fostered wars, disease, and chaos in Africa to ensure we control the diamond trade and other precious resources necessary for tech and weapons of war. We control much of the wealth in South Africa, which is why we helped South Africa become a nuclear power so that we could destroy blacks if we were truly forced to share the wealth of those stolen lands. Israel remains one of the biggest arms dealers in the world.

Racism is built into our religion, culture, and history. That is the irony we must confront if we are to rescue our humanity, our dignity, and our spirituality.

We reclaim our humanity by confronting these truths. We more effectively fight anti- Semitism by having the courage to be honest about what we have done and are still doing. Our past suffering doesn't give us the right to make others suffer.

What karma are we storing up for ourselves when we have done so much wrong for so long? What has been hidden will always come to light. We are not the 'chosen,' but we can still choose. If it's not already too late.

All my love,

Daniel

THE WEDDING

I received a letter one day from a relative in Nigeria. Before I even opened the letter, I had mixed feelings about what it would contain.

We'd been to Nigeria a few times since Dad passed and had very mixed experiences. We'd met some nice people who expressed a genuine mix of awe, curiousness, and joy that we were the children of Stephen. To the elders in particular, where we're from, Dad was, and still is, a revered and legendary figure as spokesman for our village and lead support for Nigerian expats in London. They treated us with honour, out of huge respect for him. Their respect, in turn, only added to the sense of honour and privilege I felt to be one of his sons.

But we'd also met other relatives, who saw us as nothing but cash cows, and stripped us of anything valuable when we'd first arrived all those years ago. They were envious of our lives in the UK and wanted to bring us down a peg or two and ensure we realised that we owed them, and they were in charge now. But that was then—we'd since been freed of their grasp, and I had returned several times as an adult far beyond their control.

So, I had mixed feelings when I opened the letter, and the fact it was out of the blue made me a little apprehensive. It was from an uncle whom I didn't know too well, but who'd seemed more worldly and sophisticated than other grubby cousins. I'd liked him to a degree. He wrote:

"My Dear Brother,

How are you and the children? How are you and all our family over there doing? We hope you are all doing very well by God's grace.

My brother, things over here are very tough for our people. Many are struggling just to put food on the table each day. Many haven't been paid for the longest time, and with this Government, one never knows when this situation will end. My brother, please pray for us. With God's grace, we shall overcome these hardships.

Anyway my brother, life goes on, and I don't want to bother you with our troubles. We will endeavour to keep our heads up at all times and move forward.

To this end, I have good news, my brother. My daughter, your cousin, is getting married, and we're hoping that you can come. In fact, all of you are welcome. We will be preparing all the delicacies we know you people like from your last time here. You will do us a great honour by attending, and there are many things that we, as the men of the family, should take the opportunity to discuss.

I look forward to hearing from you soon.

Remain blessed in Jesus' name.

Your brother,
Tobias."

I was in two minds. I had no illusions about the exhausting, suf-
focating expectations that would be thrown on me once I'd arrived.
There would be relatives who would want me to sponsor their move
and studies abroad. There would be others who would want me to
provide capital for their business ideas. Still, more would want me to
build them houses and provide them with a monthly allowance. This
had happened to the footballer, Emmanuel Adebayor, but he was a
millionaire, and I wasn't—far from it. In fact, I was in debt myself,
living off my overdraft since my redundancy. But they wouldn't
want to hear that. As far as many 'back home' were concerned, we
were all millionaires who'd forgotten where we came from, living
the good life while leaving them to suffer and starve, who had the
power to do all they asked—if we really wanted to.

On the other hand, I desperately wanted to reconnect with my
roots. The constant racism in England meant I never truly felt at
home or at ease, despite being born and brought up in London.
Over the years, the racism was less about direct insults to your face,
which was straightforward enough to deal with, and more that it was
clever. It was much more about managers and colleagues and organisations pretending to care about race but doing virtually nothing
for years to protect their power and career paths. It was all worthy

rhetoric, empty promises, gaslighting conversations that saw black people as the real problem. It was exhausting, circular, and perennial. Nigeria offered a potential way out from all the lies and spin about tolerance and diversity that hid the reality that, in many ways, things were getting worse.

I longed to build a house by the river Niger, to chill and read and not to have the seemingly endless burden of being seen as a threat. I wanted to spend more time 'back home,' learning more about my father, my culture, my history in the very villages and towns where it all began. A big part of me also wanted to return as the conquering hero, the prodigal son who'd been born in the 'land of milk and honey' but remembered who he was and brought back blessings for all our clan. Part of me really wanted to be able to provide the houses, the businesses, and the sponsorships.

But deep down, I knew that no matter how much I gave, it would never be enough. I was caught in a bind: when I gave, it was never enough; if I didn't or couldn't, it was said I didn't care.

Family in London were divided too. Some didn't want me to have anything to do with relatives they saw as grasping and mendacious. They reminded me of the visiting Nigerian priest, a fellow Catholic who'd befriended mum and tried to fraudulently use our family home as collateral for a loan, the seemingly devoted relatives who'd ran off with mum's life savings, the dodgy distant cousins asking for golden elephants, the kidnappings and armed robberies targeting visitors that were rife. I shared all of their scepticism, suspicion, and scorn; I knew all the dangers—but I still wanted to go.

The wedding was only of marginal interest to me; it was bound to be a marathon affair conducted in a language I had yet to grasp, centred around endless eating and drinking. I'd be colossally bored for most of it. But I wanted to explore the possibilities of setting up some kind of haven there, of maybe developing business contacts and friendships with people I could trust, people who could make repeated visits worthwhile, pleasurable and safe.

Some family members agreed; they said it was a good opportunity to reconnect with that side and see how the land lay. Others even talked about the sense of duty and responsibility we owed our relatives, that they had a right to some expectations of assistance because it was my grandfather's funds back in the day that had allowed my father to make London an outpost, and the intention all along was that the wider family would benefit from what they had initiated and established. This was the strongest argument for me, tapping as it did into my sense of leadership and responsibility.

I bought a ticket with a large loan I cashed to take and help the folks back home. I flew out to Nigeria with a mixture of excitement and trepidation. I hadn't told them when I would be arriving or leaving, as is the basic security precaution many visiting Nigerians take. I landed in Lagos and walked out of the airport to be hit by the familiar wall of heat, smells, and sounds. It was strangely comforting. I laughed as the mini cab drivers outside, spotting the 'rich foreigner,' pounced and fought over my luggage to take me wherever I wanted for a 'good price.' I was just about to enter one of the familiar, battered yellow wagons when I heard a firm voice above the din call out: "Excuse me, my friend!"

I half turned to look to my left, not completely sure the hail was for me. But it was. I recognised the man as one of the elderly friends of my father. His hair was white now, and he was held up by an elegantly carved cane—but it was the same man. I walked over with a smile, glad to see a friendly face. Years ago, he had been chief of police in our province and had taken me to the cells to see poor souls who would one day be executed. I took both his hands in mine and gave a slight bow of respect. He smiled and nodded, but I could feel a strange tension in him.

I said: "Good afternoon, sir. It is very good to see you after so long; I hope family are all well…are you waiting for family?"

"No, not at all—it is good to see you, and my family is well, thank you…I have been waiting for you, and I'm glad I caught you—you must go back. They are planning to kill you."

My head rocked back in shock: "I'm sorry, sir, what do you mean…who is planning…I don't understand…what do you mean they're planning…who…what's going on?" I was babbling in confusion. I felt a chill of apprehension despite the heat.

He took me farther to one side and explained that he'd received information from a frightened relative of mine about plans to kill those relatives who came from London and use our deaths to lure funds from remaining family in the UK.

"Some of our people are very foolish…they have no scruples and think that by killing the goose, they can extract all the golden eggs in one go. I beg you; go back now and forget about them."

I studied him closely. There was no mockery or mischief on his stern face, but his eyes retained their kindness. I remembered when we had first met and the shock in those eyes when he was told who I was, quickly overshadowed by a distant look of deep sadness as he remembered my father.

I looked downwards for a long while.

Finally, I looked up and sighed deeply.

I thanked him and offered him the money I brought. He refused, but I insisted. I turned to walk back into the airport. As I walked, I heard him speaking softly and looked back. His head was down, lost in thought, slowly shaking from side to side.

"Oh, Stephen…Stephen…" he said.

The Delivery Company no. 2

Our next delivery was to a Met police officer in a southern suburb of London. Our research showed that he'd come from a military family but joined the police after seeing what constant deployments had done to his parent's marriage.

He lived in a large, semi-detached home with his interior designer wife and three teenage children. Therefore, we needed a few trusted accomplices to help us kidnap the entire family and drive in a convoy of six cars to an isolated woodland location.

All five had been tranquillised and placed in the boot of our cars. At the location, we pulled them out and checked that the zip ties on their hands and feet were in place while we waited for the effects of the drug to wear off. They woke to find torches in their faces. The Met officer was the first to notice we were all armed.

"Listen, I'm sure it's me you want; please just let my family go." We stayed silent. "Listen, if it's about those arrests I made, I'm truly sorry." His wife and kids stayed quiet, hoping Dad could talk them out of this nightmare. "What happened in those arrests?" I asked.

He told us all about how he had a few colleagues beat up a group of black kids, breaking a few bones and charging them with assault. I said, "That's not what you're here for, try again." The cop looked at us, then at his family, then back at us. "Okay, okay, then it was the money I took in the drug sting, right? Listen, it was a one-off; I was stupid, but please don't hurt my family over this."

"Wrong again," I said. "Last chance." The cop hung his head for a few moments. "Will you let my family go?" he asked. "Depends on what you say," I said. He paused again for a few moments then told us all he'd shot and killed a black colleague because he'd threatened to reveal his extensive links to the drug trade. His family looked at him in shock.

"Well, this has all been very interesting," said my partner, "but the truth is, none of this is relevant to why you're here." He told them they were on the Government list of those who had been compensated for losing their slaves in 1833. The family didn't seem surprised—they knew. "Didn't you care?" I asked them all. No one answered.

I thought for a few moments, then I spoke: "There were numerous roles in the business of slavery and one of them was the slave-maker whose job was to break the will of the slaves by acts so foul they transmit the horror into the very DNA of the slaves who witnessed it, so they would reinforce the need for obedience for generations to come." I looked at the teens: "I bet they didn't teach you that at school, did they kids? Let me show you one of their party tricks."

We took one of the teens and attached each arm and leg to four of the cars, so he was spread-eagled as if on a rack. We turned the engines on, and each driver started to rev the engines, suspending him in the air about a foot off the ground. The cop and his family screamed and shouted, pleading for us to stop.

I fired my gun in the air, which gave the drivers the signal to go full throttle. We repeated the process for each family member then drove away. We didn't want to keep our next client waiting.

A HIGHER FORM

Dear Comrade,

We have both been union reps for more than 20 years, but in all honesty, I have never been more concerned about the hostile, aggressive, and frankly racist behaviour of some of our black colleagues. To describe them as having chips on their shoulder is not a term I would use, but there seems to be no better way to describe their behaviour.

Some of them want to start a 'Black Staff Association,' which they say is a necessary support group because of this organisation's 'institutional racism.' This, of course, is utter nonsense based on dubious evidence at best. Our colleagues in the police may have had troubles based on a few bad apples, but to suggest we, in this Service, tolerate racism on an institutional scale is a shameful, disgraceful slur and does their cause no credit. Their ingratitude, lack of respect, and misunderstanding of so many issues is astonishing.

For example, some of them claim our record on challenging alleged racism within management is poor, but they forget that these cases are notoriously difficult to prove. They say we are too close to management simply because we enjoy their hospitality on occasion, but again they fail to see that this is entirely necessary to gain an insight into management thinking for the benefit of our members and good industrial relations.

And it's completely unfair for them to say we only indulge in rhetoric rather than action on race issues when only last week you said so magnificently in our Annual Report: *"We continue to do everything we can to celebrate diversity, learn the lessons, consult stakeholders, and invite a broad range of opinions in our efforts to welcome debate and constructive dialogue on what of course are vital issues of concern in our diverse and multicultural society, in the full acknowledgement that while we have made great strides and come a long way, we are keenly aware we have a long way to go."*

I fear your words fell on deaf ears.

Too many of their number simply fail to understand these things take time. The impatience (and in some cases, outright impertinence) of some black colleagues is of growing concern to many white members of staff who rightly bring attention to the fact this is all beginning to cause damage to morale and racial harmony across the organisation. Some of the blacks have taken to going to lunch in groups, making one wonder what they might be up to and creating even more tension across the board. It's a disturbing sight, I can tell you.

A few of the women have been intimidated to the point of tears by some of their aggressive looks and threatening tones. It was only right that we alerted management and had their contracts terminated for the safety of all concerned. Regrettably, I have had to do this many times over the years, particularly with black men who do not seem to understand how expressing forthright opinions on race frightens many white people, especially white women, who may have experienced all manner of violence. Thankfully, most blacks are grateful for the opportunity this Service affords them and demonstrate the right attitude, but there is clearly a persistent minority of troublemakers who are causing extreme concern.

What has escalated these matters to a clear emergency is the fact that some of these malcontents are now demanding more representation in the most senior positions of our union.

I have tried to explain on countless occasions that our long experience of trade union practice means we are uniquely placed to defend our members' interests and that any leadership contest would only destabilise the union and play into management's hands. The truth, as so many leading comrades have said, is that many blacks simply do not understand or respect our superior grasp of socialist theory and practice. They do not understand that class issues must always supersede narrow racial concerns, and if that means whites will always be above blacks, then that is simply the natural arithmetic of socialism and democracy.

This essential fact reveals that blacks agitating for 'self-determination' in such groups are almost by definition anti-white and anti-union. In the final analysis, and if not nipped in the bud now, they could easily grow to become an existential threat to us all. In these circumstances, and in your absence, I took it upon myself to activate our emergency procedures and alert the Grandmaster at our Masonic Lodge.

Our beloved Grandmaster assured me that if we continue to provide useful information on the threats these blacks pose, then at the right time, they would be neutralised. This was deeply reassuring. We are incredibly fortunate that our beloved Grandmaster, in his wisdom, has revealed to us a higher form of socialist Brotherhood the blacks and the masses cannot comprehend. Yet, in his infinite generosity, he offers a select few, even blacks, the opportunity to be initiated into this higher knowledge.

But Grandmaster alerted me to the *Guardian* newspaper of the 25th May 2019, and one classic example of the ingratitude and stupidity of even so called educated blacks. He was referring to an article on Michael Fuller, the UK's first black police chief. This is the final paragraph:

While a serving police officer, he admitted he was approached to join the Masons. "It's just not in my nature to join a secretive organisation. I was aware they do a lot of good charitable works…I was also aware that in the lodge I was asked to join, there were judges, police officers, but there were also criminals. I said no way. That was my only dealing with them," Fuller said.

The Teachers

The teachers were in one of their nightly meetings in the basement. They'd given strict instructions not to be interrupted. There was a mixture of feelings in the room: some were angry, others were frustrated, most were frightened.

The problem was the black boys. They were proving more and more difficult to contain and control. It wasn't always said, but the teachers all knew subjugation, not education, was their primary task with this group.

All the teachers were Heads of Department, each with decades of experience. They and their front line staff were being bombarded by black students who brought to their attention a seemingly never ending chronicle of black achievement from the blacks of Ancient Egypt to the present day. Today's story was of a Jamaican who had invented a car powered solely by water. The boys were targeting the entire curriculum and producing solid research that showed black achievement went far beyond anything any teacher was aware of or wanted to discuss.

The Heads had hoped to pacify the boys during a hastily convened Black History Month, focusing on staples such as Martin Luther King and Mary Seacole, along with the usual sprinkling of sports and entertainment types. But the boys had laughed off their efforts as tired, tick box attempts to show a concern they didn't have. The boys were becoming politicised at a rapid rate. No one knew how or why.

The Heads tried another familiar tack. Mr Curtis, Head of PE, launched colourful campaigns laden with incentives to try and lure as many boys as he could away from their research and activism into sports. For years, steering black boys into sports and athletics had been a tried and tested strategy to keep inner city black kids in check and bin their academic potential.

But the boys were suspicious. The boys researched the experiences of generations before them and were horrified. They vowed never to allow themselves to be limited or defined solely, or stereotypically, by their physical gifts. They began to boycott school teams and organise their own sports events outside of school control. The boys now launched into a wide-ranging analysis and critique of how low expectations and stereotypes from school and society had decimated several generations of young black boys at crucial stages of their development.

The Heads, increasingly desperate, now decided to play their best card—they dramatically escalated the rate of school exclusions. Exclusions, even more so than sports, were the weapon of choice for Heads who recognised what was to be done about the 'black problem.' Exclusions killed three birds with one stone: they got rid of the problem, improved their position on school league tables, and herded the problem out onto the streets where gangs or the police claimed them, followed by prisons and cemeteries. Vital to the smooth operation of exclusions were white female teachers.

The negative stereotypes about black males they often brought into school were magnified now that they were in close proximity to them. Thus, for decades, it became the norm for black boys to be accused by them of aggressive or sexually threatening behaviour and to receive the most draconian punishments schools could devise. The Heads now gave extra encouragement for white females to escalate their attacks on the boys. Black exclusions soared.

But the black boys hit back. Their research on white female teachers had anticipated this move, and they now brought black pro bono legal teams into position backed by parents, educationalists, and experienced community activists. Soon, local media ran the story. Most Grime music stars deeply empathised and helped add music festivals to the boys' sports portfolio. Events were monetised all year round to provide funds that helped turn a local issue into a national one.

Most of the national media framed the issue as disruptive and dangerous black boys on the rampage. The police were urged to crack down and help restore order. Arrests soared, and black boys began to add to their already huge numbers in youth detention centres. Undeterred, the boys continued their campaign and education in prison and soon began to transform the mentality of black inmates.

However, the funds they had raised began to be depleted by legal fees. Their parents felt they had no choice but to join in the protests in any way they could. Many were spurred by the memory of their own first-generation parents who, blinded by Empire propaganda, were unable to accept schools and policing could be so racist and blamed them as children. Now they drew on those experiences and pain, calling on parents nationwide to support them. It was mostly black people across the country who answered their call—they seemed to sense this was a decisive moment. Cash and all manner of support flooded in. Black parents everywhere withdrew their children from school en masse in solidarity, pooling their limited resources to organise home tuition, using retired teachers and many who had been sacked by the mainstream for speaking out in support of the boys. In tribute and recognition of their sacrifice, they decided to use the black boys' research as the foundation of an entirely new curriculum.

Black churches nationwide, who had long stood silent on the sidelines, whatever the havoc being wreaked in the black community by white society, now came on the receiving end of heavy criticism from within their own ranks. Many church leaders desperately concerned at their rapidly dwindling power and finances, finally opened their doors to destitute families being evicted from their homes because of a white backlash from landlords, banks, and employers. Many of the new black schools also found a new home in churches, increasingly taken over by supporters and relatives of the boys. The new curriculum they used asked serious questions regarding why they had been so passive in the face of all the challenges affecting the black community for decades. A new liberation theology swept through many churches, giving the activism the boys had sparked a voice in pulpits everywhere and raising that spirit to a revolutionary fervour.

The hunger for change was relentless and soon gave way to a quest for the spiritual traditions that existed amongst black people before the Christian Holocaust. Some churches began to experiment with meditation and yoga. Other church leaders closed shop rather than allow their once obedient parishioners to practice what they considered 'pagan abominations.' Their ignorance and intransigence created a 'blacklash,' accelerating the church takeovers. Many now broke from the shackles of Christianity, what they now called 'the slave-master's religion.' They researched and began to practice the ancient religion of their ancestors, involving rituals and chants that only increased their power, insight, and new converts. With new blood of all ages swelling their ranks, the churches were physically rebuilt in the shape of pyramids to become the African temples of old, dedicated to the resurrection of African spiritual and economic power. Rituals alternated with fundraisers, business forums, and countless community initiatives, alongside daily markets selling African food, medicinal herbs, clothes, and books.

White nationalists, ever on the alert for threats to their alleged supremacy, began to firebomb the new pyramid temples. Black street gangs responded by offering to act as security and literally fought fire with fire. They wanted revenge for those killed and injured and sensed a new positive role they could play for the community. They patrolled the streets on bikes and used their networks to identify and deliver lethal punishment to racists the police couldn't or wouldn't find. The praise they received from the black community shifted their mindset, and they moved from just protecting the temples to venturing within. They were welcomed as heroes and were astonished at the hive of activity within. This all inspired them even further.

The gangs took advantage of all on offer. African revolutionary warfare and martial arts were popular but so were the huge range of black businesses and scientific ventures they were able to join that focused on the upliftment of the black community. They excelled in the incredibly supportive environment and transferred their street smarts into thriving businesses, employing many of their friends returning from prison. They turned their street patrols into sophisticated community safety, outreach, and prison teams that channelled huge numbers of black youth into the businesses and study they themselves had profited from. This created a loop with a life of its own that grew massively across the nation in a very short time, attracting huge international interest. Police now found it almost impossible to provoke the youth during abusive stop and searches. Youth, and even adult prisons, began to be empty of black inmates.

White support for what became known as 'the black revolution' increased dramatically. Huge numbers were astonished, inspired, and desperate to help in any way they could. Many studied black history for the first time. Many whites created parallel groups and societies to support the boys, their families, and black communities everywhere.

One of the most secretive but significant of these groups was a society known as the 'John Brown Martyrs.' They had embarked on a deep study of all aspects of slavery and had been horrified by what they discovered. They were shamed to the core that slave-masters, not slaves, received compensation at the end of slavery—right up until 2015. Some were SAS, deeply remorseful for the atrocities and secret black ops they had been ordered to commit against African governments and their people. They were desperate for a path to redemption. They took their group name in honour of John Brown, the white abolitionist who enlisted his own sons into a do or die armed insurrection against American slavery, shaking the entire slave-holding American South to its core and ushering in the American Civil War that led to the end of slavery. They called themselves 'Martyrs' to emphasise the lengths they would go to righting the wrongs committed against black people. The John Brown Martyrs formed small, virtually impenetrable, networks and cells, infiltrating Freemasonry and through them, the military, police, judiciary, and media, sharing priceless intelligence with the black revolutionaries who countered innumerable attempts to destroy them.

The black community, for so long with their backs to the wall, without hope or cohesion, had now forged a new unity based on the desire to protect their young and a spiritual revolution that had spread outwards to touch people from all races and walks of life. They were now generating wealth and power once unimaginable. Buoyed by their domestic successes, the revolutionaries now massively expanded their international reach and links abroad in a new phase known as the 'Toussaint' or 'Two Saints' strategy, named to honour the sacrifice of Toussaint L'Ouverture, who led the first successful revolution against slavery in Haiti, defeating Napoleon in the process—and Malcolm X, probably the most powerful black revolutionary leader and orator in American history, who had sought to internationalise the struggle against white domination. Black people worldwide had followed the developments in the UK with astonishment, and the incredible rush to learn from and replicate that revolution reached new heights, particularly across the Americas, but most of all, in Africa itself.

Black representatives from across the globe met in Africa to form African councils to coordinate and accelerate the black revolution sweeping the globe in numbers that even exceeded the mass Pan African movement of the great Marcus Garvey in the 1920s. The West fought back hard with the usual ploy of attempted coups, assassinations, and biological warfare in the form of their manmade diseases. However, the John Brown Martyrs anticipated and internationalised their units in step with these developments and formed specialist units that prevented, targeted, and neutralised their efforts and informants. The Martyrs spread chaos and disinformation in the ranks of Western military and intelligence, causing widespread disillusionment and division, rendering them almost completely ineffective.

The African councils were noted for their integrity and dedication to the needs of the people and freed from age-old Western attempts to divide and rule, began to supplant regional then national parliaments, spreading like wildfire across the African continent. Soon, the wealth of these nations was truly back in the hands of ordinary African people. Western economies collapsed, inverting the economic world order. The Africans, now with the combined wealth of their land, spirituality, and unity, rebuilt a new spiritual world order rooted in humanity's most ancient and wisest creed of balance and interdependence known as 'Maat, the 11 laws of God.'

But what of the teachers? They were discovered dead. Beheaded. All cameras and surveillance had been disabled, so no suspects were ever caught. Their school became an African temple, and the boys returned as teachers, Heads, and African World Council members.

THE EVIDENCE IS CLEAR

People go to Spiritualist churches for a variety of reasons. Some are curious and feel the pull of the unknown. Some are fearful and want to see if it's the work of the devil as they've been warned by the paedophile cunts running the Christian churches. Some come with an open mind after speaking to a partner or friend. Many come for an answer to their grief over the loss of a loved one. Many, too, enjoy the social aspect and treat it like a night out. To receive irrefutable evidence from a skilled medium that your loved one lives on in the spirit world and sends you their love is a great gift and a priceless confirmation of our immortality.

But very, very few understand that the spirit within them that is their true self brought them to this arena because it craves growth, awareness, and expression in the physical realm.

The essence of all the messages received in such churches is that we are essentially spirit beings given temporary possession of a physical body that our spirits might learn and grow through the challenges of this worldly realm and become stronger and wiser in this life and the next. This means that our spiritual growth is the true purpose of life, our real reason for being here, and the only growth that counts when all is said and done.

But for many, there is no attempt to dwell on the significance of this revelation and what it might mean for daily living, so their spiritual health is poor. This omission is reflected and repeated in the absence of personal responsibility that many take for their physical health.

But here there is an omission in church provision too. This is because in most, if not all, spiritualist churches, there is no real program for spiritual growth, no strategy to assist and assess spiritual progress, no clear map charting the way upwards to spiritual heights. Spiritualist leaders themselves say their churches exist mostly to provide evidence of the afterlife. But what then? *Evidence is not enough in relation to what we came here to do.*

Thus, even church attendees fortunate enough to receive a comforting message leave without possession of a viable, engaging plan or path forward that allows their spirit to truly rise and grow. This omission means that most Spiritualist churches and their congregations remain stunted in their growth, their vast potential restricted. Instead, they stay mired in petty politics and egos rather than creating and executing inspirational plans that increase their connection to the Great Spirit within.

The search for a 'viable, engaging path' for our spirits to fly should be the primary concern of us all. Without it, we drift and can never find peace. The evidence is clear.

THE POLICE OFFICER'S WIFE

Dear John,

I'm leaving you. And I want a divorce.

I'm taking the kids. I've cleared our joint bank account. And as you can see, I've got rid of all the furniture. Sounds a bit harsh, but no harsher than what you did to that black kid.

What you didn't realise was that he was a friend of our son, so we got the full story from his perspective—not the usual police lies you and your cop mates put out to the media.

We went round to see him, and he told us again how you beat and strip searched him, how you racially abused him and charged him with assaulting the police. What shocked me was that he and his family weren't surprised. They said every black family they know has had a bad experience with the police. We talked all evening. His dad Richard's a researcher—he backed everything he said with overwhelming evidence. I felt ashamed that I'd been one of many in society who'd sided with the police when deep down, I'd always suspected there was something deeply wrong about the way they treat and view black people.

But I'd never really bothered to look into it.

Looking back, I was proud when you first joined the Force. But we both underestimated how deep their racist culture is. They ended up changing you. You got sucked in and desperate to join the Freemasons like so many of your colleagues. You took to spending all hours with them at the pubs and clubs, desperate to please, to fit in. You changed so much.

I tried so hard to talk to you. I tried to raise the issues behind knife crime, but you became a snarling neanderthal like so many of your colleagues—"More stop and search! Lock 'em all up! More police! More prisons!"

You've forgotten they're kids, for fuck's sake!

The reality is *you're* the cause of all the chaos. Black kids don't trust the police because you've abused and humiliated them and their parents for decades. Sometimes you've literally got away with murder. The kids know this. They know you don't really give a shit unless it's a white kid. They saw how you set up that Tory minister, Andrew Mitchell. They worked out that if you could do that to him, then they don't stand a chance. Despite all the Police talk about 'learning the lessons,' they know you see them as primarily a problem and not really a part of society. They sort things out amongst themselves in terrible ways because police racism has helped deepen their lack of hope, self-hatred, and anger. They turn that anger inwards and towards each other.

I tried so hard to talk to you about all this. That what you did was wrong. I tried to show you all the evidence of police racism, all the research to show your strategy is counterproductive because it alienates the very people you need help from. That you're being used as agents of control who see black people as the enemy within. That you've changed so much. But you denied it. And you write anyone off who criticises the cops as anti-police lefties and anyone who tries to help them as 'fucking liberal do-gooders.'

You don't listen to me anymore. You shouted at me and slapped me for the first time. And the last. I know where this goes if I stay.

I don't trust you anymore, I don't respect you anymore, and I don't love you anymore. To me, you're capable of anything to keep in with your cop mates and get promotion.

After our divorce, I'm going to work with Richard and the race equality campaigner, Stafford Scott—Richard says he's the best in the business. I'm going to work for justice for Richard's son and children like him. I'm going to make sure our children know the truth and hopefully do a lot more to change things than we ever did.

Susan,
your ex-wife

THE DELIVERY COMPANY NO. 3

Our next delivery was to an elderly woman living in a north London council flat. Our research had shown she had received the compensation for years but chose to live a humble life in the area she grew up in. We used two trusted white partners for this job.

"Good evening, Mrs Levy. Please don't be alarmed. We're from the Treasury and just want to make sure you're receiving all the compensation you're due." They showed her fake IDs, and she let them in with a smile of appreciation.

Over a cup of tea, she told them excitedly how the 'nigger money' had paid for everything—from homes in the disputed settlements of Israel, to new homes for her children, to university fees for her dozen or so grandchildren, and endless gifts for friends and neighbours.

"That's wonderful!" our partners said, smiling at each other and her. "Do you have any concerns that it was your slave-holding ancestors who received this compensation and not the slaves themselves?" "Oh no, no, no," she said. "Not at all! You must understand that these people are not the Chosen like we Jews...no, no, no, they've been condemned by God Himself to be slaves forever—it's in our holy scriptures...they're the cursed descendants of Ham, and it was God's will they be enslaved to good people like us, so they could learn the ways of civilisation...it was our duty to enslave them; they should be grateful…thankfully, my children and grandchildren understand all this and haven't been corrupted by all this politically correct nonsense about these days."

"Quite," our partners agreed. "And will they be visiting soon?" "Yes! It's my birthday today, and they'll all be here celebrating— they're such good kids." There was a knock on the door. "Excuse me, that must be them." It was us. We pushed past her and dragged her back into the centre of her living room. "Excuse me! What the hell…how dare you! I'm going to call the police!"

We bound her to the chair while she continued to protest. "Call the police!" she shouted to our white friends. "I'm sorry, madam, but these are our partners, and they're here to make a very important delivery." "What on earth are you talking about? Call the police at once…this is an outrage…I'll have you all arrested…get your filthy black hands off me, you animal!" We sat her on a wooden chair and bound her hands and feet before tipping her and the chair backwards onto the floor.

"What are you doing, you black bastards! You'll pay for this! I'll see you never see the light of day again in your life…do you know who you are dealing with? I'm Miriam Levy…"

Our white partners looked at us apologetically and then back at her with unconcealed rage. I handed over the large plastic bag I'd brought. Our partners had locked a face clamp into position to keep her mouth open. I explained to Mrs Levy this was exactly the type used in slavery to punish outspoken slaves. She struggled and cursed as best she could. Mrs Levy's nose wrinkled at the foul-smelling bag they dangled over her, then with her eyes widening in recognition and shock, she began to plead in simpering whines. My white partners emptied the brown contents down her throat. She gagged, coughed, and choked, but they continued for several minutes until the wriggling and choking stopped and she lay still—her eyes still open.

We retreated back to the delivery van and watched the house. It wasn't long before the birthday party arrived, a seemingly endless stream of relatives happily rushing into the flat. We heard the screams. They were all still in. I pressed the detonator. We drove away to meet our next client.

THE BUS RIDE HOME

I'd spent the day down the Southbank. I had a lovely time casually strolling, people watching, taking in lunch and the sights.
I headed to the bus stop to take my bus home. It was still a nice evening, so sitting at the top watching the people go by was almost an extension of the lovely day I'd had.

Halfway home, a black man and his three mixed race young children sat close to me. The man sat directly in front of me with a young boy about 3 years old. The youngster sat on his inside next to the window. The two other children were slightly older, a girl of about 6 or 7 and a boy maybe a year older than her. They sat together on the seat directly to his right.

Shortly after sitting down, the man began to point women out on the street to his children. He pointed out that this woman was sexy, that woman was a fat bitch, the other woman was a skinny wretch, and so on. He encouraged the children to identify with what he said, and the girl copied his lead saying, "Look at that sexy bitch," and so on to her brother, and they all laughed. This went on for several minutes, and I have to confess, I was shocked. I'm no prude, and I've probably said similar things in my mind, but this was a father with young children encouraging his children to objectify women out loud on the top deck of a packed bus.

Because I was directly behind him, I could smell the drink on his breath, but the slur in his voice was clear and loud to everyone. This fact only made things worse in my mind because he was in charge of children. I wondered if the mother knew he was like this. I wondered if she was partly responsible if she did and still partly responsible if she didn't.

Perhaps I shouldn't have, but as a black man myself, I felt a tinge of shame at his behaviour, but I wasn't quite sure how to approach things because he was there with his kids. He carried on for what seemed like ages, getting more graphic and nasty with his descriptions.

I decided to gently tap him on his shoulder. My intention was to simply say something along the lines of: "Is that really appropriate with young kids?" as gently as possible so as not to embarrass him.

I tapped him on the shoulder, very gently, and said "Brother" to signal straight away that I had no malicious intention as I initiated my intervention. I didn't get the chance to say anything else.

As soon as he felt my touch on his shoulder, he turned and exploded in anger: "That's fucking assault! Who the fuck do you think you are? The white people haven't got a problem, but it's our own black people making a fuss! You see what I've been trying to say to you kids? It's our own fucking black people who are the problem! I've told you you can't trust them! Listen, if I see you in the street, I'd fucking do you, you fucking idiot." He continued with his tirade for at least another ten minutes.

Again, I was in shock. I looked around to the other passengers and shook my head, hoping just for supportive non-verbal acknowledgement. But as anyone who's been on a London bus knows, most people don't really give a shit. And even if they do, most don't want to get involved. Everyone's head was turned the other way. One young black guy in his twenties actually looked at me with reproach and mumbled I was a 'wasteman,' i.e. a waste of space, because I had touched the drunk father.

On and on the drunk father ranted at me, making threats, cussing and cursing me out to his kids. They became silent, and the older boy began to cry. The girl pleaded with her dad: "Please, dad...not again, dad." But he didn't stop.

By now it was night, and the bus only had a few stops and a few hundred yards before it terminated. Mr 'Wasteman' got off the stop before me. I got off at the next stop a few yards on and ran back in his direction. I caught up with him and from a few feet behind, said, "Excuse me." He half-turned but carried on walking. It was nighttime, after all, and he was streetwise. "Excuse me," I said, again trying to keep pace with him, "I really didn't appreciate what you said."

"Who the fuck are you? Get the fuck away from me, you cunt!" He'd stopped in indignation. I pulled out my gun. The silencer was already attached. The streets were deserted. His eyes widened as he felt the first shot in his chest. The second shot to his head closed them.

I ran on to where the bus terminated and circled for a few seconds before I saw the father with his kids.

I followed from a safe distance and saw the house he entered.

I went round to the back. It wasn't long before I saw lights going on and off upstairs, and I assumed the kids had been put to bed. I waited another hour to be sure. Downstairs, the lights were still on, and I heard adults talking above the adverts on a TV. I climbed in through an open window into the kitchen. I entered the living room.

"Please don't be loud—I just want to talk."

The dad, and I presumed mum, looked at me in open mouthed shock. I stayed at the door. For some reason, I addressed mum: "Your partner was drunk and swearing at me in front of your kids, he…"

"WHO. THE. FUCK. ARE. YOU? Get the fuck out before I call the cops!" Mother said, slow and deliberate, trying to take control although there was a tremor in her voice. Dad was blinking the drink from his eyes and squinting, trying to remember where he knew me from. Then, his eyebrows shot up in recognition. He stood up, reached for an empty bottle, and started to swear, all at the same time.

I raised my gun and fired into his left leg. He shouted in pain, stopped mid-swing as if he'd hit a wall, dropped the bottle, and fell sideways back down on the sofa across mum, blood pumping across them both. Mum screamed but quickly caught it in her throat and covered her mouth. I hoped the kids were still asleep. I stood opposite them, blocking the TV.

"I was trying to say dad here was extremely abusive on the bus to me and other women in front of the kids."

I knew they were still in shock, but I was hoping for some show of remorse or regret from either of them. He just moaned in pain and looked at her to save them from the situation. Mum tried again:

"Look, I don't know what the fuck you want, but my kids might be down in a minute, and he's gonna bleed out if I don't get an ambulance—so will you please just fuck off and leave us all alone!"

I sighed and raised my gun again. I shot them both in the head. I made my way out the back then called the police, disguising my voice and alerting them to the kids upstairs.

I must admit I was relieved to find out later that the kids were allowed to stay together and were fostered to a good family. They had been my main concern all along.

The police had no leads on all three killings. Both they and the press soon lost interest because there were no pretty blondes involved.

I had no regrets. I'm still angry all three had been so rude and disrespectful.

THE RAGE

In a new job with a trendy charity, I quickly discovered that white managers occupied all the top positions, so white staff knew they had more clout, credibility, career progression, and job stability than their black peers. Black staff were too cowed and frightened to express an opinion that might run counter to their white colleagues.

There seemed to be a weird over representation of young white women in the office as well.

They loved the edgy, diverse nature of the town where we were based, with its history of black culture, night life, music, bars, and trendy ethnic eateries everywhere—but couldn't actually give a fuck about the massive struggles of black people, either historically or in the present day. They wanted to enjoy the fruits of diversity but couldn't give a shit about the adversity that led to it. Race and racism, though a burning issue in the country, was never seriously discussed in the office. An event in the town centre to commemorate the thousands of black soldiers who fought and died in world wars saw only two of us from the office attend, but at a Black Lives Matter march, which shut down the town centre, I saw no colleagues at all.

The smug, cosy sense of superiority and privilege amongst white staff, their complacent and complicit ignorance on live race issues, their dismissiveness and indifference to our proud history and daily struggles, truly drove me nuts.

One day, I brought to the office a black entrepreneur, a former offender who had turned his life around. He'd published books about his experiences and started a social enterprise to help other offenders stuck in a pattern of serious and repeat offending. I was impressed with him and had briefed my colleagues about this individual and how he might help us work with some of our most difficult cases.

I walked him into the large office over to the section where my particular team sat. So far, the only people in my team at their desks were two black guys and one white woman. They faced us but had their heads down in front of their computers.

As we arrived, my black colleagues immediately looked up and acknowledged our presence. I did the introductions. The white girl didn't move. She didn't look up. She didn't involve herself. She didn't acknowledge us or show the basic manners and interest my black colleagues did. I silently noted it and continued our conversation professionally.

What I felt inside, though, was entirely different: the racial dynamics in the office had given her permission to show the most enormous disrespect. White management had created the environment for this sort of daily, casual insult from white staff until their sense of superiority was so ingrained that it had become as natural as breathing. Black people simply didn't register as deserving of the most basic courtesies. White staff had been shown and taught subconsciously and subliminally that black people just weren't as important as white people.

I felt the four of us black guys, with probably a century of experience between us, with several lifetimes worth of knowledge, with each of us at least 20 years older, wiser, and more relevant to the job than she could ever be, had been dismissed, trashed, and disposed of in a second, reduced to inconsequential rubble *without even a look.*

We just didn't matter. I'd spent my entire career and most of my life challenging racism, painstakingly building my self-knowledge and pride as a black man in a society that after centuries, still branded the likes of me as a problem, and here I was being shown that everything I believed in, everything I had achieved, worked, and fought for, all that I had risked, and how I defined the very essence of my being, didn't deserve even the briefest of acknowledgement, didn't deserve even the pretence of respect.

Reader, I suspect you will never understand the rage I felt—but it is important you try.

Before anyone had time to react, I had lifted her by her throat with both hands and threw her out of a nearby open window several floors to her death.

Being on death row now holds no fear in me at all. In the moment of her death, I felt more alive and justified than I had ever been, and each day, I cherish the memory.

THE BOY WHO WOULDN'T TALK

Apparently, the doctors said he had some form of autism or Asperger's, I never remember which, and his mum said he could talk, but he just chose not to. I was probably the closest to him from our church because our mums were best friends, so I used to visit a lot. It was shocking to be in his room; it was more like a library, and every available space was stacked with books; his bed actually rested on them. Most of us kids were glued to our phones and TVs and iPads, but there was no screen of any kind in his room. I couldn't interest him in any games, but it was actually more interesting to watch him than do anything else when I was with him. He could read so fast, and he took loads of notes. It was really odd, like watching some kind of mini professor.

One day at church, the minister was asking people to come up to the front and testify how the Lord had changed their lives. So boring. But it was mum's favourite bit because it gave her hope that Jesus would do the same for her. Anyway, on this particular day, no one had much to say, and the minister was just about to move on when the boy said: "I'd like to say a few words if I may." His mum nearly fell off her chair. I was so shocked, I wasn't even sure it came from him. Everyone looked in his direction in stunned silence as he walked up to the lectern; even the musicians had stopped playing. I wasn't supposed to, but I switched on my phone to record it, and I could see phones popping up from the adults too.

He thanked the minister and then looked out over the church. He didn't seem scared at all. Then he started:

"As adults in the black community, you have lost the respect of many in my generation. This is because you cling to the slave-master's religion like a child holding a teddy bear. It has the whiff of the bizarre and the ridiculous. The people who enslaved us would never give us that which would save us. Even as children, we can see this. The whites have made their contempt for us clear over centuries and killed our leaders, such as Marcus Garvey and Malcolm X, who did more than any white Jesus to show us the way forward. In looking to white gods to save us, you have abandoned the first principle of parenting, which is to protect your young, your future. We, as a people, are facing a quiet genocide at the hands of whites whose principal tools of deception and violence are plain for even young children to discern.

"Beneath your impotent spirituality is a capitulation, a surrender to materialism that mimics the concerns of our modern day slave-masters. So, you dress in your Sunday best but give your worst in building for our future. Where are the black multi-national, national, or even local businesses that could provide us jobs and security in a white world that works to relegate us to the bottom of almost every scale of social and economic disaster?

"Where is the effort to develop a unity amongst our people that would bring our latent genius to the surface and channel it into nation-building that would astonish the world once again as in Ancient Egypt? It lies dead because you adults believed the lie that we were idol-worshipping savages with no coherent spirituality or history of achievement before the Christians 'saved' us. The empty white rituals you mimic here every week and your dereliction in our communities show that you believe that lie, have been defeated and re-enslaved by that lie, have been emasculated and humiliated by that lie, have fed us, your children, with a diet of such lies. A lie that many of the whites admit was a lie.

"We children see, feel, and sense this emasculation, this daily humiliation, as we watch the world you helped create yet fail to truly participate in. We wonder whether you will ever wake from your slumber. We wonder whether you *want* to wake from your slumber. You seem to prefer the numbing comfort of self-deceit to the challenge of opening your eyes to what in your souls you know needs to be done. In this self-imposed prison of the spirit, you betray yourselves as well as us. You show us that you no longer have the courage or belief to protect yourselves—never mind us. So we, as misguided young, develop misguided ways to protect ourselves and survive because you have offered us the guidance of the slave, the defeated, the blind, the informer. Consumed by the fear bred into you, you retreat into the barren womb of this church, this religion, with your teddies in hand that you call the word of God, given to us in exchange for our land, our precious inheritance that now nurtures, builds, and makes real their dreams of dominance forevermore.

"You have shamed, disgraced, and insulted the Ancestors on the slave-ships that gave every ounce of every part of their mind, body, and souls that we might survive to live better than this. You have shamed, disgraced, and insulted the countless black leaders assassinated here in the West and in Africa who fought till their last breath that we might survive to live better than this. You worship their heroes, not ours; you bow to their saints, not ours; you kneel to their leaders, not ours; you study their scriptures, not ours; you build their futures, not ours.

"Like so many Jews in Nazi Germany, you stay silent to the truth and collaborate in our genocide for the fake silver pieces of consumerism that rots your souls to leave you mannequins instead of men and kin. You've thrown us, your lambs, to the wolves because you are the sheep of their flock. We bleed because you let them lead. You've sacrificed this precious life and countless opportunities to rise for a Jesus who will never come. Jesus never came when we were slaves, so why should he come now when on the surface at least, we are rich and free compared to the bottomless horror and barbarity we endured for centuries? We saved ourselves then and must do the same again now. But you have abdicated your leadership, squandered the fabulous inheritance of Malcolm and Marcus to kneel to white saints and white men who plot your demise on earth as you pray to them in the skies. What must we say of those who look to their enemies to save them? Who worship those who depose, despise, and dispose of them?

"Our Ancestors are watching, soon to return in their droves to usher in a new world they will helm. You either repent to them and change now or become as dead leaves that must be cut away to allow new growth to be born. You either search your souls and re-trieve your true purpose for our people, or forever be condemned as wilful collaborators, who even in death, will bear the grim agony of endless regret."

He walked out of the church.

We were all numb with shock.

I felt real fear in the church that day. The church was never the same, we were never the same, and we never saw him again.

The Deathly Sleep

At 10 years old, I was the best story writer in my primary school class. I was proud, and a little embarrassed, that almost every week Mr McLean would choose my story to be read out to the whole class.

In secondary school, this talent wasn't encouraged. Like so many others, my creativity was lost to the demand of slavishly following the curriculum so that when we left to become wage slaves, we could do our bit to maintain the status quo.

When I entered the world of work, my job was to write reports to a particular formula. There was little room for creativity beyond the odd turn of phrase that one had to be careful wasn't too immodest.

In my spare time, I went to a few writing classes and signed up for a distance learning course. But for whatever reason, I just couldn't summon the enthusiasm to write anything beyond a few hesitant, exploratory paragraphs.

One day at work, I was contacted by an academic to write a chapter for his book. My piece was to be on a speciality he didn't possess, and I was an acknowledged expert in this field.

What should have taken me a few months ended up costing me over a year and a half in angst and worry. It dominated my thoughts night and day. It was classic procrastination, nothing more. I knew what I wanted to say; I was just worried about how it might be received by my colleagues. Worrying about what others will think is the first mistake in the writing process.

I eventually finished the piece, and the book never found a publisher, so all that worry was so much wasted energy. And even if it had and people hated it, as a writer, that should not be your primary concern. Your primary concern should be to speak your truth, as you see things from your soul. All else is fake and easily spotted as such, and all of us rightly hate fake writing much more than we hate that which has been written from a place of honesty.

Decades passed again, then one day, I decided to try a few free sessions of life coaching. The coach was a woman who seemed to share my perspective on life, but who was much further along in terms of living her dreams.

She was warm and funny and pushed me to write stories, albeit very short ones, for the first time since school, almost forty years earlier. What I felt most from her was a genuineness in her encouragement and a strong belief in my talent. I valued her time and warmth and wanted to live up to her expectations, so I wrote my stories each day, even if they were in the form of long phone texts. When my time with her ended, so did my stories. I was clearly one of those types of people who needed someone caring and consistent to push me.

More long years passed, and I felt the lack of creativity within me like a parched man chained to a dry well. It frustrated and ate away at me subconsciously, souring my relationships and any sense of peace. Anger at others and at life usually had its true source in the bottom of that empty well.

One day, I found a new partner, and we seemed suited in a way I hadn't experienced before. She was incredibly intuitive but equally practical. She shamed me with her work ethic but was never anything other than totally supportive of all my dreams and ideas. But I still didn't actually do anything. One day, several years into our relationship, she had a premonition of total disaster if I didn't give it my all to achieve my writing potential. By now, I had very good reason to rely on her insights, so I was deeply shaken. I think I started to write the same day.

I began to write stories that expressed all the rage and frustration I had felt for so many years. All the slights and insults and disrespect and injustices I'd experienced, heard of, and felt empathy for found voice in my characters. Though initiated by my partner, I wrote the stories primarily for me. I didn't pull any punches and didn't write to please or persuade her or anyone. I wrote stories I wished I had read, stories that I'd never read and was unlikely to because they were too controversial, violent, or shocking. But however fantastical and unlikely, they all contained more than a grain of truth. They were grounded in my experiences, insights, study, and what I knew or felt to be right and true. *My* truth.

Writing from my heart and soul wasn't just the cathartic experience that many writers talk of; it allowed me to feel and experience the fact that I was finally walking the path of my destiny, and that it was truly in my hands. Writing reawakened the creativity in me that we all have, and all must use. If not, we risk looking back at the end of our lives and coming to the awful realisation that we wasted it.

Being creative in a way where you speak your truth allows you to tap into your reason for being here. It gives the world a unique perspective that acts as your contribution to the rise of us all because the ripples of truth never fade. It allows you to tap into the limitless insight and bounty of the universe because Spirit is always looking for avenues and pathways, through people on Earth, to help bring us to our senses.

All the excuses I made in my life not to write led to a very real form of death. Writing has woken me from that deathly sleep, just in time.

THE BLACK STAFF SUPPORT GROUP

I'd been away for many years, and I was curious to know what the Group was up to, hopeful there might be exciting new developments, maybe to connect with old acquaintances.

I went with an open mind, not to judge, not to criticise, just to observe, to hopefully enjoy some of the old camaraderie, perhaps in the back of my mind to see if I could find a few like-minded souls.

I looked around and saw many of the old faces—the usual suspects. They looked weary, more cynical. There was no warmth in the room. Their souls were cold. There were no new faces, no new blood coming through making their presence felt, setting bold new agendas. The old crowd didn't seem to notice, or care. It was older, but no wiser.

I'd seen one good old friend and expressed my joy at seeing him in my usual unrestrained, raucous manner. I was told to keep the noise down because it might upset nearby colleagues—white colleagues. I felt my anger quickly rise. I said, "Fuck them—they wouldn't think they had to be quiet for us; they wouldn't give a damn about us." I was shocked that there was still the old fear of upsetting whites, the same self-policing and deference, even when we were meant to be enjoying each other's support and company.

One of the leaders talked about his vision for the future, but they were empty words I'm sure even he didn't believe. The members talked about their experiences. They spent a lot of time patting their own backs, clearly glad to be in a room where naked careerism was valued, expected, invited. It was odd, surreal, tinged with a nauseating familiarity.

On and on they droned about the various problems and impediments that others had placed in front of their precious, all important careers. Others nodded sympathetically, sharing stories and advice about how best to climb up the greasy pole, how best to ingratiate themselves with white power, how best to survive and thrive away from the black brethren beneath them in ghettos—that it was the height of ambition to escape. The whites were their lifeline now, their workplace Jesuses. Those who had bought new houses and cars were congratulated and quizzed on their purchases, a tinge of envy if it was better than theirs, but something to aim for, or to exceed, if possible, and then bring the good news back to the Group about their upwards progress, to show everyone how they were making it.

These people had created a bubble for themselves. A parallel universe as barrier and protection from the real concerns of ordinary black people. They didn't talk about finding ways to support the communities they had come from, whose sacrifices had made the space for them to be there, who had a right to be remembered and supported. There were no plans to support their kinfolk suffering on the streets at the hands of the police, the black kids being excluded from school in droves. There were no plans to make even a token gesture of support at the many marches or campaigns for justice. As had been the case for so many years, the key issues on their agenda were their careers, their pay, their conditions, their cars, their holidays, their clothes, their hair, their socials. They didn't want to talk or think about those they'd left behind. New members only joined because they were about to be fired and expected someone to magically save them. Or they wanted help to get promotion, then they'd fuck off, never to be seen again. "I did it for you," I remember one such fucker saying.

I wanted to kill them all.

They didn't talk about who they were as black people; they didn't talk about where we should be going as a people or the serious threats we faced on so many critical fronts; they didn't have any vision of how they could be a force for change that would better the lives of their community or who we could link up with who was. They didn't talk about other black achievements apart from their own, or other petty, parochial matters, no other events except their black-tie dinner and dances for the bargain price of £100 that would fund more talk about themselves, again. If you raised wider, or urgent, racially charged issues, they'd look at you like you'd suggested rummaging through their grandma's knicker draw. Tiresome, cowardly, but plausible sounding bollocks would be raised about how it wasn't the right time, or the right issue, or the right fucking weather. You could hear their white bosses talking—or their white handlers in the intelligence services. Same thing sometimes, I'm sure.

When forced into public statements, their leaders came across as stilted mannequins, spouting over-academic phraseology as if the real pressing issue was to show how many degrees they'd acquired. I realised they saw even these as networking opportunities, invaluable in raising their profile and career prospects. They would go back to the support groups and be congratulated on their performance, told how they were senior management material. And they were right because they had mimicked their white masters in saying all the right things with all the passion and conviction of dead dodos, so devoid of true concern that on a subliminal level, their words transmitted that black lives didn't really matter. We were dying in droves here and abroad. We were being humiliated and abused in the schools, by the police, and in prisons on a daily basis. The Group said very little and did even less. At least the Black Police Association had the balls to say recently that the Met was an unsafe place for black people to join. But 'concern' had been expressed by the seemingly plausible and representative cunts in our Group, so the public could all go back to business as usual. I thought if there was no passion or anger or rebellious fervour from these fuckers, then why should white people be bothered?

And I wanted to kill them all.

At the next Group meeting, nothing had changed, and I realised it never would, that these people were of no use to us, that if they had never been born, it would be actually better because then the truth about white institutions would be revealed, much like how the black community had virtually boycotted police recruitment campaigns, exposing their utter failure on diversity and prompting their own leaders to admit it would take a hundred years to reflect in the city. At least it was out in the open. We all knew the police were racist, murdering cunts, and contained many, *many* who deserved to die. But here, black staff had let white managers off the hook; their craven campaign to kneel before their white masters for career crumbs had made the organisation look good, had attracted unsuspecting new recruits to the mind-numbing frustrations of gaslighting racism on a daily, almost hourly, basis.

Today, I'd brought a large bag. They were surprised, to say the least, when I pulled out a fully loaded assault rifle.

Let's just say the next 5 minutes weren't pretty but were very necessary.

THE PARTY

The most senior police officers in the Met police were gathering for a toast at HQ to celebrate their progress on diversity. They were all white.

The champagne and canapés were just being wheeled in, but Tessa Henderson couldn't join in the party mood.

She was a senior officer, too, but felt deeply uncomfortable with all the laughter and mutual back slapping. Despite the head of the Met being a woman and a handful of women making it to these rarefied levels, she knew it was still a boy's club—a white boy's club.

She knew that all the years of media spin, solemn pledges to change, diversity plans, ethnic recruitment drives, 'zero tolerance,' and smiling ad campaigns had achieved virtually nothing. And the whole game cut no ice with the black community, who for decades, had had to deal with the daily humiliation, insults, contempt, and brutality of a force that privately was in near total denial. She knew the truth from the inside, as they knew on the street, that the Met couldn't give a damn but had to pretend it did.

Her role meant liaising with black families and Forces across the country. She'd seen everywhere how officers of every rank still saw black people as criminals to be controlled rather than legitimate members of the community to be served. Any internal attempts to merely reflect on this briefly were dismissed as 'politically correct thought control' or 'fucking social worker type naval gazing' by the Police Federation—the police officer's union who fought any efforts towards progressive change as if they were attempts to introduce ebola.

Tessa knew the senior officers present were drawn from this culture—it was in their DNA. Many had made their reputations cracking black skulls, and those with black deaths on their record had actually enhanced their careers in the eyes of many of their colleagues. But over the years, they'd learned how to play the game on race. They'd mastered how to talk the talk and to effortlessly charm with the right sound bites to the right people at the right time.

Privately, she knew they couldn't give a fuck. They'd told her as much because their numbers meant she was no threat—she knew if she grassed, they could arrange an accident as easily as ordering a cuppa. Their imminent, fat, taxpayer-funded pensions were all that mattered. As far as they were concerned, it was white men who were the endangered species, it was white male officers who needed all sorts of protection from the PC madness. Anyone who thought differently obviously hated cops.

She desperately wanted to leave the party, but it would attract too much attention. In any case, the Commissioner was about to speak.

The Commissioner rehearsed the rhetoric she'd later repeat to the *Guardian* newspaper. She said the Met has transformed and is no longer institutionally racist, that the headline finding from Macpherson was redundant: "I don't feel it is now a useful way to describe the service, and I don't believe we are. I simply don't see it as a helpful or accurate description." They cheered and drank to her health, someone started to sing 'God Save the Queen' and soon everyone joined in, swaying from side to side, and as they did so, revelling in their Brotherhood.

Tessa saw her moment to make her escape. She felt desperate to get into the night air, to drive home, to take a long shower.

She bumped into an elderly black canteen assistant on her way out. She knew he was one of many black support and cleaning staff about to be made redundant so their jobs could be outsourced to a white firm, linked to one of the officers inside. There'd be no champagne parties or fat pensions for them. Suddenly, her eyes blurred with tears.

"Ma'am...are you okay?" His ID badge said his name was Errol. "Y-yes...er, Errol...thank you." "I know you don't drink, ma'am, so are you sure everything's okay?" "Yes, I'm sure...thank you again."

Thankfully, her car was parked just outside. She put the key in the ignition and had begun to pull away when an odd thought occurred to her:

How did he know I don't drink?

She ran back into the hall, but she knew what she would see before she got there.

Errol stood amongst the bodies. He looked up as she burst in.

"Some of us can't forgive, ma'am...they hurt so many of us, so much, for so long."

THE PRESIDENT

President Wesley Jackson, the second black president in US history, had two guns pointed at either side of his head by two different people with opposing demands.

In front of him was an open briefcase with a red button that was the trigger for nuclear war. It could only be activated by fingerprint identification from the president himself.

Both gunmen were four-star generals at the top of the US administration, though they had opposing views as to the threat Russia posed.

General Goldberg believed intelligence clearly showed Russia was about to make a nuclear strike that would annihilate the West. He urged a pre-emptive strike that would save the country and the Western world.

General Warren believed the intelligence was seriously flawed and came from unreliable sources. He was adamant a pre-emptive strike would trigger a response that would utterly destroy both sides.

The generals were brothers—twins. Brought up since birth by two different families, they had nonetheless embarked upon the same vocation, each believing they had been marked for high destiny. After discovering each other late in life, they had sworn to never be separated again and to defend each other's life to the last. But, independent of each other, they had made odd simultaneous decisions to use their security clearances to enable them to smuggle in weaponry and place the president in an impossible dilemma.

The president had an internal dilemma neither general was aware of. His biography omitted to mention several lost years in his youth where he had undergone a secret rite of passage deep in the heart of Africa. He had volunteered to undertake a mission to destroy all white men, at whatever cost to himself. The rituals involved in his initiation had empowered him with tremendous abilities, only a small fraction of which he had needed to call upon to enable him to become US president. But his commitment to that mission had been compromised by the fact that he had fallen in love with and married a white woman, who bore him three children that meant more to him than he ever could have imagined.

All three men were drenched in sweat.

"Sir, I'm going to have to insist you press that button NOW!" said Goldberg.

"Sir! If you move an inch, I will have no choice but to shoot you, sir," said Warren.

In such moments, time warps and slows.

The president's thoughts switched to the years he spent in Africa before the initiation, of the total humiliation of grinding poverty that had forced him and so many others to literally eat dirt. He remembered the strange diseases that had wiped out entire communities, causing sufferers to die in unspeakable agony. The old men who had initiated him blamed the white man for many of their ills. And they were right. He had been so proud to be chosen. The old men saw a rare determination and selflessness in him and had dared to whisper to him their most secret and ancient prophecies. The president's thoughts switched again to his lifetime in the West. For the majority of his life, he had seen how his African American brethren possessed combined wealth now unimaginable to those back home, but who had done so little to alleviate the suffering of their brothers and sisters in the Motherland. Their lack of unity and spiritual grounding had rendered them almost worthless, unworthy of redemption, along with the whites.

"Sir!" shouted Goldberg, who now took the safety off his gun and cocked the hammer.

"No, sir, do not move, sir!" said Warren, who did the same.

In these last seconds, the president thought of his children, his wife, his mission, the cost of it all, the necessity of it all, life for all, death for all, secrets and whispers. His head, which had been so still, now suddenly tipped forward, and the generals who had been taut and tense to beyond breaking point simultaneously fired, killing each other. He felt them fall to the ground—and pressed the button.

As thousands of nuclear warheads from both superpowers burst into the sky seeking cities and continents to destroy, the president smiled as he remembered the solemn whispers of the old men:

'Our kin in the land of the Pales will fail and die in sin,
Our son from the land we hail midwifes our Light within.
Though death from skies will fall, and earth removes her stain,
The blacks, whose Light shines tall, shall rise again and again.'

OUT OF AFRICA

I was with a couple of close friends in the canteen of Howard University, the historically black university in Washington, D.C. We were depressed. Another unarmed black man had been killed by cops; we were being incarcerated and used there like slaves in numbers that far outstripped our presence in universities; Democrats and Republicans both used our suffering as a political football for votes, as they had done for years, and there was no great black movement or individual that we could pin our hopes on.

Black Lives Matter was a significant new development, but as students, we'd done our research and knew it hadn't actually reduced the rate and number of killings. It had just highlighted to the world something most whites considered new but what we, as black people, had gone through for centuries in 'the land of the free and home of the brave.' We'd get shot or choked by a cop in cold blood, the world would be horrified for a moment, then after the usual character assassination, they would blame us and go back to their online shopping, their Netflix box sets, celebrity gossip, and the latest football or baseball fixtures. We felt hopeless and more at risk than we'd ever felt in our young lives. We knew that out on the streets, our education would count for nothing at the hands of a police and media who seemed to see us as little more than escaped slaves who should rightfully be in prison to make white America great again, to make white America safe again.

"I swear I fucking hate this country," my buddy Omar said as he was close to tears with an anger and frustration we all felt. "You don't hate this country," I said, "You just hate the injustice in it." "Yeah," said Wesley, the third in our trio, "Remember, this country belongs to us more than anyone; we even built the White House, for Chrissakes." "Yeah, so the Man could live fucking high on the fucking hog," Omar added. "But at least we had a black president; we were eight years in power," said Wesley, smiling. But he was being ironic. He was doing his best because we all knew that Obama had done nothing for black people. Everyone else got their piece of the pie: gays, women, Latinos, but Obama had done nothing for black people. We'd watched Dr Umar Johnson's YouTube video, 'Obama Helped Every Group Except the Black Community,' and as much as we didn't want to believe it, we'd checked and couldn't fault his research: everyone but us got their share, despite the fact that we had paved the way for everyone else and built the wealth that everyone else ate from. Dr Umar exposed our political and historical naivety, despite us being in the hallowed halls of Howard. It was another bitter pill to swallow.

"How the fuck do we change this shit?" Omar was shouting, but we didn't tell him to pipe down. We couldn't answer him. We didn't have anything to say that would make it better.

We'd sat in silence for a while, wrapped up in our own thoughts, when I got a text from my Dad. I'd been dreading it. We were only days from summer vacation, and he wanted the whole family to visit our folks in Africa for a few weeks. I couldn't think of anything worse, and Dad knew it. We'd argued for weeks. I was adamant I didn't want to go 'back home,' as Dad said, to meet relatives I'd seen enough of and couldn't care less about. And there was no KFC for miles. But Dad was paying for the wheels that helped me get laid, so I knew I was going to have to take an 'L' on this one. My heart sank as I read through his text citing the details of our flight, then I sat up in shock: Dad was offering to pay for my friends too. I guess he'd been more affected by the arguments than I'd thought. The guys were stoked; they'd never been to Africa and saw it as the ultimate adventure. Omar, in particular, couldn't wait to get away: "We're going to the Motherland, bro!" It was good to see the smile back on his face.

The first thing that hit us when we came out of the airport was the heat. It had been a while since I'd last visited, and I'd forgotten how the sun almost seemed to be closer than back in the States. Dad had arranged for a minibus and driver to take us to our village. It took six long hours. I remember the really young kids selling food and drinks along the journey. They looked desperate and hungry. For some reason, I couldn't shake the feeling that that could have been me. Omar and Wesley had been quiet for most of the trip; I could see they were trying to take it all in and process the new colourful chaos of the crowds, traffic, smells, noise, and tastes of the strange food.

Finally, we arrived at my Grandfather's large, dilapidated house deep in the bush that Dad had made just about fit for human habitation. I looked at Omar and Wesley, "We're not in Kansas anymore," I said, and we all laughed. There was something oddly comforting about being 'back home,' as Dad called it, but I couldn't put my finger on it until Wesley said: "You know, I haven't seen a single white person all day." It was still daylight, and we were immediately surrounded by hordes of barefooted village kids curious to see who these exotic new strangers were with their weird clothes and ridiculous footwear.

The following morning, we had beautiful young village girls in colourful robes, not much younger than us, serving breakfast of pounded yam, plantain, eggs, and pepper soup. It wasn't quite the Colonel's recipe, but it more than hit the spot. I looked at Wes and Omar, and I could see they thought the service was as delicious as the food. Dad was on the veranda with us but stood a few feet away, smoking his pipe and looking into the distance. I knew he was up to something when the pipe came out.

The next day, the minivan and driver arrived. Dad left the rest of the family behind to take just me and the guys on another long drive to the coast. We arrived as a few fishermen were just bringing their nets in for the day. I'd been there once before, years ago, but I never remembered seeing an island in the distance that Dad said we were going to row to. It all felt a bit odd, and I felt a chill of apprehension, but I didn't want to alarm the guys, so I shrugged it off and trusted that Dad knew what he was doing. Why Dad couldn't get a boat with a motor, I couldn't understand. He sat back smoking his pipe while we rowed towards the island. As as we got closer, I could see it was thickly forested, virtually jungle. Omar and Wes loved the strangeness of it all, but I noticed the few fishermen we passed looking at us with concern at the direction we were heading in.

We tied the boat to a tree, and out of nowhere, Dad produced a machete. Thankfully, we weren't about to be offered up as some kind of sacrifice—we all still had college to finish, after all. Instead, Dad used the blade to hack through the undergrowth, and we followed the path he made, dodging all kinds of weird insects as we made our way deeper into the heart of the island. I'd forgotten how fit Dad was and how he'd grown up in these conditions. We all used the gym regularly back at Howard to impress the girls, but we still struggled to keep up with him.

By the time we reached a clearing several hours later, we were all drenched in sweat, our clothes were ripped to shreds, and I suddenly realised we hadn't brought food or water. We hadn't seen a single soul as we cut through; in fact, we hadn't heard a thing, not even birds. At this spot, we didn't even see or feel insects anymore. The centre of the island seemed totally uninhabited, lifeless, and the light was now fading. Dad walked a few yards away from us and sat down in the middle of the clearing. He closed his eyes and began to chant, using words I'd never heard before. Wes and Omar looked at me as if I knew what the hell going on, but I was clueless. "Man, this ain't funny anymore," said Wesley to me. "Bro, I'm tired and hungry—and what the fuck are we doing here?" whispered Omar. I agreed with both of them, but I didn't know what to do.

At that moment, the strangest thing happened: a young girl, no more than 9 years old and wrapped in a black robe, emerged from the thick bush and walked towards my dad. He opened his eyes and said, "Hello, mother." We all looked at each other to see if we registered the same thing, then back at the girl. We were too shocked to speak, but we all thought the same thing: "Mother? What the fuck is going on…?"

The young girl sat on Dad's lap and looked towards us, smiling. Dad looked relaxed and beckoned us forward, but we were too scared to move. The girl didn't say a word. She produced odd looking leaves, some sort of berries, and a water gourd from a knapsack she had around her shoulder. Dad said that we should come and eat. We were still terrified, but the combination of hunger, thirst, and Dad's reassurance meant that we crept closer until we were a few feet away from them both. I could see she wore a strange necklace made of tiny skulls. I counted fifty. She suddenly stretched out her hand with the leaves. Instinctively, we jumped back. Dad could see we were terrified, so he sat her down and brought the leaves, berries, and water to us.

The leaves and berries tasted surprisingly good, but we couldn't understand how it made us feel full. And the water gourd that we passed around never seemed to run out. Dad explained things to us as we ate and drank. We weren't surprised when Dad told us that Grandma was some sort of super powerful witch, but we felt a tremor of horror when he said she had died before I was born and lived in another realm. Apparently, she was able to visit our world and take the form of any being she chose.

Then he dropped another bomb. Grandma wanted all of us to stay. For seven years.

We wanted to get up and run for our lives, but we couldn't move. Grandma continued to smile. Dad continued to talk.

He said the movement of distant planets and stars had aligned in a particular way for the first time in countless thousands of years, allowing the spirits of high priest ancestors from the Ancient African civilisations of Egypt that we're descended from to work with Grandma to reverse the damage to the Earth, now at a crisis point, and to usher in a new reality based on spiritual principles known as the '11 laws of God.' He said white men had violated those laws, triggering a reflex action in the universe that was already under way and was irreversible. He said that thousands of years ago in a previous life, Omar, Wes, and me had been high initiates of the Temple of Amen and had pledged to repeatedly reincarnate together as family and friends over time and space to help facilitate these changes. He said at this very moment we could still choose what we wanted to do.

Our mouths were open, but we couldn't speak. Grandma stretched out her hand again and gave Dad tiny black seeds, which he put in each of our mouths. As soon as the seeds touched our tongues, we saw, in visions that seemed to last for hours, the truth of all that Dad had told us.

We stayed for seven years while Grandma taught us things that we can never reveal. Grandma was much more powerful than we could have possibly realised. When we went back to the US, we realised that only two weeks had passed.

There were still some days when I would wake up and think it was all some amazingly realistic dream. One such day, I went to speak to Dad, who was smoking his pipe out on the porch while working on his laptop. I was startled to see a magpie bird sitting on his lap. He showed me the article he was reading. It was from the online *Guardian* newspaper based in England. The headline read: 'The infertility crisis is beyond doubt.' Dad told me to look closer, I read on: *'News last week that sperm counts in western men have been cut in half confirm what experts already knew. The real problem is that no one knows why.'*

THE DELIVERY COMPANY NO. 4

We sat in the Professor's office. My partner faced him on the sofa while I sat in the Professor's high-backed chair behind his desk. It looked like a chat amongst friends, but we'd disconnected the alarm systems, taken his phone, locked the door, and had lookouts strategically positioned outside.

The Professor was a renowned academic from Oxford University. Our research suggested he had numerous connections with very bad and very powerful people, so we were taking no chances. The Professor seemed calm despite our silenced pistols aimed quite unkindly in his direction.

We'd explained our reason for being there, but he'd waved his hand dismissively, saying: "I knew something like this would happen one day." I was intrigued. He saw the question in my expression and continued: "I've studied patterns in nations, empires, business, nature, weather, crops, birth rates, and so on…most conform to rhythms and cycles that have a degree of predictability. In this instance, your actions are portents of the end of our cycle, that is, the Western cycle, of dominance. There are many other portents, of course: the declining birthrate amongst Western males is a significant one that most can't understand. But those of us with an esoteric bent have anticipated this for a while."

"Interesting," I said. "That might well be the case, and if so, it's overdue and very welcome. But at this point in time, we're just concerned about the here and now and your assets." "Yes," he said, "you mentioned I was on the list of compensatories. You're aware, of course, that Africans indulged in slavery, which itself has existed since time immemorial." I said I was aware, but that African slavery, while not to be minimised, was minute in scale and of a different nature compared to the industrialised barbarity involving countless millions that Europeans presided over where slaves were no longer considered human beings, had no rights whatsoever, and were bound for generations without end—until they themselves made the whole system ungovernable.

"Hmmm," mused the Professor, a nervous twitch beginning to form at the corner of his eye, "you've obviously done your homework. You're not just thugs, after all. What do you intend to do with the money?" I sighed. I said that we had projects we were funding in Africa and the UK that targeted the communities most affected by the ongoing legacy of slavery. "And catching people like you doesn't come cheap," I added. "I can imagine," he said. "It's no piece of cake taking me unawares with the precautions I took— you've done very well," he said with a rueful smile.

"Well, it's been a nice chat, but I'm afraid we're going to have to wrap things up now." A glimmer of fear flashed across his face, but he managed to stay in control and continue stalling. "Before you act too hastily, might I offer you some information?" I said, "There's not much I imagine you could say that would save your life, but make it quick."

He talked about the work of the black academic and activist Dr Umar Johnson. His evidence pointed to a well-advanced conspiracy to drastically reduce the population of black people in both Africa, as well as the West, through secretive sterilisation programs, biological warfare, false vaccination drives, and many other deceptive tactics and strategies. "They want to remove your people from the face of the earth if they can," he said, "and I have the documents to prove it." He retrieved them—they looked genuine. I was familiar with Dr Umar's work and knew the documents would be invaluable. I sent them to him the following day.

"Although we're grateful, Professor, this is not going to be enough." We stood up and raised our guns. "Wait!" he said, arms outstretched and a sheen of sweat popping on his brow.

He said he knew of a family that had profited more than most from slavery, a family of vast, deliberately underestimated wealth that still had ties and control over many of the countries and peoples affected. "The Royals?" I asked. "Yes, yes, yes," he stammered. "I guessed as much," I added, "but how does that fact help me?" He said if I wanted to take them all down in one swoop, he had inside information that would make that possible. I said that's utter nonsense; we'd looked into it, and they're far too well protected. "True," he said, "but no plan is 100% fool proof...and you don't have the inside information I have." I said I didn't have time for games, so give me what you have, and I'll decide whether it's worth your life.

We helped him retrieve a device from his safe, and he ran it on his laptop. My partner came in close, and on the screen, we saw confidential security details of the Royals that could only have come from the very people protecting them. Me and my partner both looked at each other with eyebrows raised.

"Why would you share this information with me?" I asked, "Surely, your type would die for the Queen…for Queen and country and all that bullshit, right?" "Once, perhaps…but my work has been criminally overlooked for honours by that crew, despite numerous recommendations. They caught whiff of some nonsense about me and young boys…they've lost my vote, I'm afraid…and I deserve to live more than they!" There was a note of wild desperation in his voice. His eyes swivelled between us, searching, pleading.

I smiled at how easily these types turn to treachery against all those they profess to love. I could tell my partner thought the same because he raised his gun at the same time I did.

OFFICE POLITICS

I was relatively new to the team. I wasn't expecting my feet to be kissed, but I was about 20 years older than most of them and, mistakenly perhaps, just assumed that they'd want to learn from my decades in the game and my black history/anti-racist expertise. But they showed no curiosity or respect for my experience. I was just another black nobody. And a mouthy one at that.

In the office, Kerry was the type of white woman for whom the life or death race issues we faced as a community and a people were a very poor second to the more profound issue of how to snag her next boyfriend. Perhaps that's unfair, they didn't come second, they barely registered at all. Instead, she posed endless questions about how to be the object of male desire to the endlessly patient black girlfriend she had reduced to little more than a sidekick in her very own 'movie.'

What made all this so intolerable for me was that we were in an office which was half black, working with a clientele that was three-quarters black. Kerry was aided and abetted by white management who didn't understand the depth and nuance of daily office racism. Our white lesbian manager herself had stopped in her tracks when she saw three of us black guys go out to lunch. *We were her staff.* She knew us, but she literally stopped what she was doing with a colleague and turned to stare as we walked by, like we were off to

plan a black revolution and massacre innocent whites. *Our manager.*
It was bizarre. It reminded me of how so many white lesbians and
white women, in general, I'd met could talk for England on sex-
ism and homophobia, but their faces turned into blank, uncompre-
hending mush or thinly disguised contempt when black men tried
to explain racial office politics and the wider context that fed it. To
them, racism was some distant 80s phenomena to do solely with the
police, or America, but surely not in *our* office. And how dare you
accuse me, or us, in any way of racism or collusion!

Kerry was attractive; I won't deny that. But even though I was
an inveterate, womanising bastard, I resisted the urge to even hint
at flirting with her because I didn't want to become like one of the
white pricks sniffing deferentially around her cunt, or one of the
black guys she drained of miscellaneous technical information to
prop up her career without actually giving a fuck about their lives as
black people in a racist organisation and society. To cunts and idiots
like Kerry and our white managers, racism was always 'out there,'
and raising it in a way they didn't find acceptable was an act of
aggression that marked you out as troublemaker to be watched and
gotten rid of at the first opportunity. As black people, we couldn't be
ourselves. Black staff often went out for lunch together just to get a
breather away from the toxic, white, racist complacency and denial
that was choking us all.

What got me, too, was how white women didn't feel they needed to do any extra work or study to improve their professional practice and understanding of black clients and colleagues—but if I'd

joined a predominantly female organisation with predominantly female clientele and shown no interest or knowledge on female issues
and been outraged when confronted, I'd have been marched off the
premises by security before lunch on my first day.

As with most white people, even those with degrees, they
couldn't be bothered to do any basic research on race before they
spoke to you. They expected you to educate them without any con-
cept of how exhausting it could be re-explaining stuff you'd thought
was established years ago. As a black person, you were constantly
having to spill your guts to these lazy cunts, who then dismissed
what you said as 'just an opinion.' The same women would dis-
solve into tears if you did the same to them on women's issues. They
threw out racially ignorant remarks like confetti, and you'd have to
carefully decide which ignorant shit you were going to tackle at the
risk of being seen as aggressive for correcting them with an experience or piece of evidence that differed from their holy sanctified
ones as white cunts.

One day, Kerry was chatting to me and another black guy, and
race came up in conversation. Kerry asked the two of us in a miffed
tone: "Why is it when race is mentioned, the focus is always on black
people?" It was as if she resented the attention we occasionally received for the horrendous treatment we received. Of course, racism
affects Asians too, but she hadn't thought that through or researched
the simple fact that Asians, despite terrorism, were still abusively
stopped and searched less often and treated better than black people
in most areas that were measured. As I said, her tone was miffed,

frustrated even. It was like, 'when will other people get a look in?'
It was as if when the news highlights what's going on with us, it's:
'we've heard it all before, thank you,' and if it shows what's going
on with others, it's because nothing important is happening to us.
It was as if we had control over the news, and she was confused
and resentful. Her attitude was in line with the ignorance and subtle
disrespect she and other white colleagues showed black colleagues
almost daily. The other black guy present was nice enough, but not
confrontational when necessary, like me. I'm sure she said it while
he was present as a form of protection in case I kicked off. But I
kicked off anyway. It had all been building up.

I didn't explain all of the above to her because when you're
angry, your thoughts aren't always coherent. I attacked her complacency and arrogance and dismissiveness and disrespect with both
barrels in a loud, rambling rant that shocked and frightened nearby
colleagues more used to sweeping everything under the carpet.

Nothing happened immediately. Kerry called her boyfriend
who came and sat opposite her, clearly to protect her from the black
savage who'd gone the full Mike Tyson and might strike or rape her
in front of dozens in the large open plan office—obviously. I found
out later that one white guy had run into a manager's office to snitch.
About a week later, that manager asked me what happened with a
face that said: 'I don't give a fuck what you say, you're guilty.' I
was warned that even before the incident, senior management was
thinking of getting rid of me. That didn't surprise me. No one else
at all was openly and repeatedly complaining about the ridiculous

bureaucracy and hidden race issues apart from me. I resigned that day. I knew I'd get no support from anyone. White staff thought I was a racist nutter, and black staff were too cowed to support me, but they wished me luck, relieved that they were no longer in danger of being dragged into battles they didn't want.

Looking back, I'm sometimes a bit annoyed with myself that I wasn't as coherent in my fury as I would have liked to have been—but I'm intensely proud that I was the only one in the team prepared to consistently take a public stand against the racist arrogance and complacency of the whites, who were used to having everything on their own terms.

THE SINS OF THE FATHERS

To my fellow Christians and the millions watching around the world:

You will all want to know why I did what I did. Many have called it incomprehensible, an abomination—but allow me a final audience to share my motives, then feel free to judge.

At first, I was incredibly proud to be ordained the first black Pope. It was an incredible honour for me to be summoned from my humble Archdiocese in Africa to be honoured by my brethren gathered from around the world in Italy. I was so proud to receive this honour on behalf of all my parishioners. But then the spirit of God filled my soul, and I found the courage to say these words in my acceptance speech today:

"My Fellow Archbishops, Brothers in Christ,

"What a truly incredible honour that you have bestowed upon not just me, but all of Africa, by nominating me as the first black Pope.

"As you can imagine, I've struggled tremendously with what I should say on such a momentous, historic occasion. But in truth,

I've struggled for many, many years with the thoughts I'm about to reveal.

"The truth is I no longer believe the Catholic Church, or indeed any Christian denomination, serves God's purpose on Earth. As a Catholic priest, I have felt burning shame as the details of our seemingly endless abuse of children around the world has been revealed. I was one of those who stayed silent when I should have spoken out, who recommended brother priests be moved on instead of prosecuted, who put the Church's reputation above that of the protection of our precious, innocent children.

"I had believed that whatever our failings, our good works outweighed them, and we were the bulwark against Satan and all his confederates. I believe that no more. I believe we ourselves have become satanic and have spread our sinful acts like a virus worldwide for countless centuries. The abuse of vulnerable, trusting children is not the only indelible stain on our faith. We have conveniently forgotten what we did to millions in Africa, and we have made no real apology or amends for our many crimes there. We destroyed many magnificent indigenous cultures we classified as pagan abominations and imposed our own doctrines—all to facilitate the barbarity of enslavement and the rape of their lands for the enrichment of the Church, which of course, continues to this day.

"And what is our legacy in the cradle of civilisation? It is war, poverty, and starvation. It is the countless millions of Christians in Africa who hold on more tightly to the nonsense we forced on them than the profound wisdom and richness of their ancient culture. An ancient culture where thousands of years ago, African humanity had reached spiritual heights we can barely comprehend. Our faith, if truth be told, is but a pale imitation of their mysteries and secrets which they codified over thousands of years in scriptures, songs, and symbols that laid the basis for all the world's religions, and indeed for all the arts and sciences. In comparison, Western knowledge is akin to a child robbed of vision who has grasped but one hair of an elephant's and claims this is the entire body.

"When trying to simply discuss these issues with you, my fellow Archbishops, I was confronted with a level of denial, of complacency, of contempt, of condescension and evasion that shocked me to my core and confirmed all of my worst fears.

"What an abomination we have become that we can insist on our parishioners confessing their sins and making harsh penance while we do nought but evade and deceive and deny to avoid justice for the millions we hold in religious bondage for filthy profit. None of us is innocent, except the children, because we chose power over the truth in our hearts; we chose contempt of our black brethren over respect and honour. In some of you, I see anger at my words, anger

that hides shame and fear, for in your heart of hearts, in the spark of the divine within your soul, you know my words are true but do not yet have the courage to change. I beseech those who do have that courage to join me with others around the world who seek redemption and justice. We live in a world that cannot be saved without it."

My speech ended there. I looked in vain for support amongst my brethren. In truth, they are more accustomed to bestowing honours and praise amongst each other than dispensing the cold, searching light of truth. They are more accustomed to sharing the profits of sin in their grand abodes, in their grand robes that convey their grand titles. There was no remorse, no apology, yet they demand the same from their flocks each and every week. Their faces were contorted with anger; they rose as one to condemn, to defend, to deflect, to denounce.

They screamed in rage: "Look at all the good we do! We lifted you poor beasts from savagery with the aid of Jesus Christ Himself!"

I said we were neither beasts, nor poor, nor savages—and we had welcomed you as brothers with a naivety born of our spirituality. I said all the Christian churches took billions and gave back pennies; billions to pay for your grandiosity while we struggle and suffer and starve and die.

Security was called. I knew my time was short. By undermining their sense of superiority and jeopardising their wealth, I had signed my own death warrant.

Some outraged clerics could not wait and approached my lectern with menaces, hoping to seize me bodily for my blasphemy, my treachery, my unbearable truths. But I had anticipated their murderous outrage—steeped in their hypocrisy as I had once been. I pulled from under my unsearched papal robe a sub machine gun—a memento from the tribal wars the good Christians had instigated amongst us. A burst of gunfire towards the ceiling halted them in their tracks and bought me a moment of silence.

"Didn't Jesus throw out the money lenders from His Father's temple? Then what should I do with you for crimes that would shame the money lenders a million times over?"

I levelled the gun in their direction—some dropped to their knees in fervent prayer, others froze in shock, still more begged for mercy that they had never shown.

In desperation, some lunged towards me but were cut down with arms still outstretched. I saw each bullet as a blessing, each archbishop falling as a cleansing, their blood flowing as freely as had the tears of the wronged.

I fired again and again until there was silence. None had escaped. At last, I sat and read the words of President Jomo Kenyatta:

"When the missionaries arrived, the Africans had the land, and the missionaries had the Bible. They taught us how to pray with our eyes closed. When we opened them, they had the land, and we had the Bible."

A Children's Story

My Daddy is very silly, and he is very funny, and he makes me laugh a lot.

I'm hiding from him so he can't hear me, and so I can tell you what he did today, and you will say he is so crazy.

Last night before bed, he said that a long, long, long, long time ago in the Old Time there used to be people whose whole body was pink. Pink! Like the inside of my hand! Everybody knows there are only us brown Afriginals and always have been.

I said, Daddy, that's ridiculous. I may be only little, but I'm not stupid. He said, it's true, and he put on his serious face to pretend he was telling the truth. He's tricked me before with his serious face, but I let him carry on talking because he is so funny.

He said that the pink-skin people used to give paper with pictures and writing on it to get food and stuff. He said that they invented sticks that shooted out stones that hurt people. He said they were always trying to make bigger and bigger sticks to hurt more and more people. "Why did they want to keep hurting people?" I said. He said so they could have lots of the special paper and steal people's gardens, especially Afriginals' gardens. I laughed a lot when he said that. "How can you steal so many gardens?" I said. But he said it was true.

He said they made the whole world fight each other. Three times. "The whole world?" I said. "Yes, the whole world," he said. "How can you make the whole world fight?" I said. "Well, you can," he said, "if you tell lots of lies and have lots of big firesticks and keep trying to take people's gardens."

He said the pink-skins fought amongst each other a lot and used their big sticks to make everybody else take sides. "So, what happened when the fighting was finished?" I asked. He said there were still lots of pink-skins left. I said, "Well obviously, if they're still around, they're just going to keep fighting and make everyone else fight again."

"That's right," he said. "And they were taking all sorts of things from underneath people's gardens that was making the planet sad and sick." "Why did they do that?" "So they could move around in metal boxes that made lots of smoke." "Why did they do that? Couldn't they fly like us?" "No, they couldn't, hun. Well, they could, but only when they built big metal birds they sat inside of that made even more smoke." Dad's story had so many bits in it, I was thinking he might be telling the truth.

"Weren't there any good pink-skins?" I asked. "Yes, there were lots, but they were almost all killed by the bad ones." "How come?" "Well, the good ones kept on believing the lies of the bad ones, but the bad ones just used that as an excuse to be worser and worser until there were no good ones left, and even the ones that wanted to be good were too scared to be good."

I told Daddy I was getting bored of his story because the pink people sounded so silly and horrible with all their fighting and paper and smoke and killing. He said he needed to finish the story because he hadn't got to the best bit.

He said our Afriginals in the Spirit world were getting fed up with the pink-skins and did special magic with Afriginals down here during the third whole world fight to make sure they couldn't have any babies anymore to save the world, and those who were left had to go to a special island that they couldn't get away from so they couldn't bother Afriginals anymore, and there's still a few left, and we're going to visit them tomorrow, so you'll see I was telling the truth.

So, last night I went to bed all excited. But when I woke up, I saw Daddy at the end of my bed. And guess what? He was wearing a pink suit to pretend he was a pink-skin! And he even had a black stick! I said, "Daddy, I know it's you; why couldn't you just take me to the island like you promised and show me the real ones?" But he didn't say anything, and do you know why? Because he *knew* he should have taken me to the island.

Anyway, I flew up here before he could catch me. And it won't be long before Mummy calls us both to have breakfast, and she'll tell him off for being crazy again.

ABOUT THE AUTHOR

Chiatulah was born and brought up in 60s pre-gentrification south London to Igbo (Nigerian) parents. He attended Catholic primary and secondary schools before spending 16 months in Nigeria, having been tricked by relatives abroad. Chiatulah returned to England and obtained degrees in social science and social work before becoming a probation officer in 1991, working with serious offenders and running a variety of specialist offender groups. In 1999, Chiatulah left to establish a successful business that trains criminal justice organisations nationwide on Race Equality. Chiatulah still lives in south London with his German wife. *Black Lives Rising* is his first book.

ACKNOWLEDGMENTS

April Gloaming Publishing for the balls, appreciation, vision, and a decent percentage.

Fools will claim that my wife's relentless prodding, pleading, prompting, and pushing forced me to complete these stories. Nonsense. It was my own rugged self-reliance, spartan discipline, and clean living that won the day. Perhaps, on occasion, she cooked a few (unsatisfactory) meals that provided meagre sustenance—but that is all. The glory remains mine alone.